Hal Johnson, illustrated by Tom Mead

FEARSOME CREATURES OF THE LUMBERWOODS

20 Chilling Tales from the Wilderness

Copyright © 2015 by Hal Johnson

Illustrations copyright © 2015 by Tom Mead

Adapted from a book by William T. Cox, published in 1910 and now in the public domain, also called *Fearsome Creatures of the Lumberwoods*.

Library of Congress Cataloging-in-Publication Data is available.

ISBN 978-0-7611-8461-4

Workman books are available at special discounts when purchased in bulk for premiums and sales promotions as well as for fund-raising or educational use. Special editions of book excerpts can also be created to specification. For details, contact the Special Sales Director at the address below or send an email to specialsales@workman.com.

Workman Publishing Co., Inc.
225 Varick Street
New York, NY 10014-4381
workman.com

WORKMAN is a registered trademark of Workman Publishing Co., Inc.

Cover design by Colleen AF Venable
Interior design and glow-in-the-dark design by Phil Conigliaro

Printed in China
First printing July 2015

10 9 8 7 6 5 4 3 2 1

Contents

Editor's Note

This book is a retelling—a reimagining, really—of *Fearsome Creatures of the Lumberwoods,* by William T. Cox. Published in 1910, Cox's book is one of the few sources of mythological animals in North America. Some of these creatures you may have heard of before (if you ever find yourself passing through Rhinelander, Wisconsin, be sure to visit the statue of the Hodag) while others seem to begin and end with Cox's telling.

In this new version, the stories have been entirely re-imagined by Hal Johnson who often borrowed from other myths and lore. If you're from Arkansas, you might know about the gowrow that feasts on shadows, just like the snoligoster; if you make your home out west, you may have heard tall tales about the slim cowboy who dodges a lasso by turning sideways. Because what good are tall tales if they always stay the same? Better to pass them around, exaggerate, and embellish, so they can grow taller (and sometimes wider).

Dear Reader

The world is filled with frogs and zebras, and you have probably seen them both in zoos and dissected them both in school. But the world is filled with stranger animals, fearsome creatures too terrifying for most zoologists to understand.

I have devoted my life to their study. I am a cryptozoologist and, if I do say so myself, at or near the forefront of my field. So many colleagues have been eaten by chimeras, incinerated by salamanders, or pecked to death by barnacle geese; there is not necessarily much competition left.

The focus of my study has been the lumberwoods of North America, a land still wild and untamed at the margin, populated only by lumberjacks and their mortal enemies, the cruel trees that once tyrannized this land—and, of course, by fearsome creatures.

This book is the fruit of a lifetime of death-defying feats in the jaws—the literal jaws—of some of the deadliest animals ever to stroll across the earth, but it is by no means complete. There are many undiscovered, or half-discovered, creatures still extant on this great continent. There is the hidebehind, for example, whose most distinguishing feature is that whenever you look at it, it is hiding behind something. Pecos Bill caught one and donated it to the Cincinnati Zoo; but even then, when researchers tried to study it, the creature was always concealed behind the bars of its cage. There's not much to say about such a beast; not much is known, so I also left the hidebehind out. I left out the slink and the ring-tailed tooter. There are enough fearsome creatures in this continent to fill sixty or seventy books such as this one. I sometimes marvel that anyone makes it to the grocery store and back alive.

FEARSOME CREATURES
OF THE LUMBERWOODS

Hodag

(Imperator rex)

While he lived, Paul Bunyan served as the master of the Michigan lumberwoods; since his death, its only master has been the hodag. Three thousand pounds of pure carnivorous appetite, the hodag most resembles a bull-horned rhinoceros with a spiny back.

There are larger creatures in North America, and there are faster creatures in North America, but there is nothing that can challenge a hodag.

I almost owned a hodag, or a part of a hodag—more or less. A smooth talker named Wellborn T. Herder had a plan to capture and exhibit the hodag as part of a traveling amusement show, and he sought me out as a potential investor.

"I will invest in your scheme," I told him, "if you can answer three simple questions about Browne's *Pseudodoxia*."

"I don't know what that is," said Herder, so I threw him out the door. But he did eventually find a backer, a mantis wrangler named Constantine Vosko, and the two conspirators twirled their mustachios and discussed their plans. With Vosko's cash, Herder bought a large tent, painted outside and in with colorful, borderline realistic pictures of the hodag, breathing fire (*impossible!*) and swallowing people by the busload (*possible*). The tent fit in the back of a large truck they would take turns driving. Oh, they were clever fellows.

Herder and Vosko would roll into town with the truck's sound system blaring.

See the wild hodag! Nature's fiercest antagonist! *Absolutely not for children!*

They set up the painted tent and charged a sawbuck (that's $10) for entrance. The hodag, Herder explained to the packed house, was behind *this curtain here*, and he would be leading the beast out, in chains, very shortly—but first a description of the terror that is the hodag!

At that moment, Vosko, crouched behind the curtain, pressed play on the terrifying field recordings of the grunts and screams— the roaring! the snarling!—of a young wild hodag. Herder, dressed in the sequined cape of a circus daredevil, regaled the audience with tales of hodags ripping up trees by the roots and redirecting rivers with their great horns. And as he spoke, the sound of the hodag would reach a crescendo, until, at the precise moment, Vosco would rattle chains and shout from the back—

"Have mercy on us ALL! The hodag's escaped!"

At this point he would pull a lever and the tent would half-collapse. The terrified townsfolk would bolt out the way they'd entered, leaving Herder and Vosko to roll up the tent quickly and jam it into the tractor trailer, their pockets filled with ten-spots. No one ever stayed around to demand a refund. And Herder and Vosko were off to another town, with another group of gulls to defraud with their hodag noises and their showmanship. They crisscrossed the Midwest with this act, fleecing towns and congratulating each other.

If Herder had known that Browne's *Pseudodoxia* was a classic seventeenth-century treatise on the history of errors, especially the history of errors concerning fearsome creatures (which he did not), he would have received my expert advice; and my expert advice would have been for them to stay the heck out of Michigan.

They did not ask me, of course. And so one bright autumn day they ran their scheme in Sandlebarge, Michigan, a small town in the Upper Peninsula. Wellborn Herder was in fine form, strolling back and forth before the audience in his sequined cape. He spoke of the hodag's well-known antipathy to lemons; of the hodag's beautiful tears, which coalesce into gemlike drops, and which have been worn for centuries as jewelry by the native Chippewa; but mostly he spoke of the deadly ferocity of the hodag, and had even begun calling out a roll of the many who have lost their lives to the beast's voracious jaws. As he always did, C. Vosko hid behind the curtain and played his old tape of hodag cries. Everything was on schedule. Everything was according to plan.

Herder had the crowd on the edge of their seats with his bloodcurdling tales, when suddenly there was a great crashing noise from the back, and a cry from Vosko—a cry of pure terror, cut short. Part of the tent collapsed. *This is not the right time at all*, thought Herder, but he decided to play along. "Flee! Flee the hodag!" he cried, his face a study in feigned terror, and the audience streamed from the tent in a panic.

Herder, meantime, pushed back the curtain to snap at his partner for changing up the program. There, behind the curtain, what did Herder see? He saw Vosko, his eyes wide and his shuddering lips unable to gasp out a word.

The upper half of his body was there, but the lower half was already *disappearing* down the maw of an enormous beast.

Investigators later determined that it was a mother hodag, attracted to the sounds from Vosko's recorder, the sound of a young hodag crying.

Investigators found half of Vosko and about a quarter of Herder, but the tape recorder was never found. The mother hodag had carried it away with her.

Left behind, rather pathetically, was a small pile of gemlike tears.

Hugag

(Sinegenu coniferferus)

There are several animals on this earth that lack knees; most of these are legless creatures, snakes or fish and the like. But only the hugag has four long, straight legs that cannot bend at all. This unusual characteristic gives the beast a distinctive, lumbering gait. Some say the forests it lives in are for this reason known as the lumberwoods; others say this is a lie. But none can deny the presence of the hugag, the largest land mammal in North America.

Indeed, the diet of the hugag—tree bark and pine needles, which it strips from the trees with its dangly lips and swallows whole—coupled with its great size and prodigious appetite, risk destroying wide tracts of the lumberwoods through overgrazing. As the hugags have few natural predators, the need to control their population has been a public policy issue since the nineteenth century. But how to hunt a creature the size of seventeen President Tafts?

Lumberjacks sought in vain to dig a pit so broad that the hugag could not stride right over it on its storklike legs. They wondered if fire would work against its resinous coat (it would not). They tried shooting the beasts, but hugags are so large that bullets entering their body tire out and quit before hitting a vital organ. Even tracking the hugag is difficult as its tracks are so far apart. Furthermore, it possesses unsurpassed natural camouflage: The pine needles it eats pass unbroken through its digestive tract and into its bloodstream, to pop out through the creature's skinlike quills. The hugag is literally bristling with plants, and blends in with the evergreen trees all year long.

Can't hunt it; can't trap it.

The hugag presented a problem. Until, that is, an opportunistic lumberjack named Kennebec Joe struck upon the solution.

There are certain nocturnal species of tree that are only seen at night, and experienced lumbermen go "night-logging" to harvest them. It was on one such night-logging expedition that Kennebec Joe first saw a slumbering hugag, leaning against a tree to support its massive frame. (Because of its kneelessness, the hugag must sleep standing up, like a Frenchman.) Kennebec Joe learned to distinguish which particularly attractive and comfortable trees the hugag favored, and he began "notching" them, sawing halfway through the trunk.

When the hugag leaned against the weakened tree at night, its great weight would break the tree in two, causing the creature to fall helpless to the ground. (If you, dear reader, have ever tried to stand up without using your knees, you will know how difficult it is.)

Once the helpless beast is flailing on the forest floor, the hunter's only concern is reaching it before a wampus cat or fearsome hodag discovers and consumes it, pine needles, bones, and all. Not coincidentally, this method allowed Kennebec Joe to fell a tree with only half the lumberjacking work.

Thanks to Kennebec Joe's innovation, the hugag population fell to manageable levels. They may still be spotted in the wild along the northern banks of Lake Huron, where human life is cheap and there is no law. Locals sometimes attempt to lasso them and put them to work drawing carts or sledges, but the resin from their piney skin just gums up the harnesses. "The hugag cannot be tamed" is the motto of the Manitoba branch of the Women's Christian Temperance Union.

The most famous hugag, though, is neither on the W.C.T.U.'s medallions nor one of Kennebec Joe's trophies. Rather it is the notorious talking hugag discovered by Enoch Melanchthon in 1899.

It transpired that Enoch Melanchthon (a local schoolteacher of upright and unimpeachable character) arrived one day in the notary public's office in Hayward, Wisconsin, and swore an affidavit that he had heard a hugag speak; and not, furthermore, in the fragmentary and monotonous mode of the parrot—a cheap parlor trick!— but in complete and intelligible sentences.

The news set northern Wisconsin abuzz with excitement, and with a small degree of guilt. If the hugag were indeed an intelligent creature, capable of mastering the English idiom, perhaps it was criminal to saw through their sleep-trees; also to decapitate them and use their skin for bathroom air fresheners.

Eggheaded East Coast scientists flew (by autozeppelin) to Wisconsin in an attempt to record a hugag in the act of speech, but the only words their wax cylinders succeeded in catching were "blart" and "grah," words of arcane meaning and which some averred were not proper words at all; no one would play hangman and choose "blart."

Enoch Melanchthon, meanwhile, sat through several dozen newspaper interviews before an enterprising reporter thought to have him transcribe the sentences he had heard the creature utter. In the newsroom, Enoch Melanchthon sat at a mahogany desk. He twirled a pencil around his thumb. He had to concentrate hard to remember the exact wording; also he was not the most literate of men. Painfully and laboriously, in crude block letters, Enoch Melanchthon slowly scrawled out what he remembered the hugag saying. He wrote:

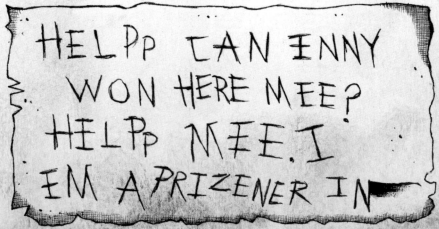

He got no further before the room cleared. The reporters were busy grabbing up saws and axes and heading into the lumberwoods to notch trees in hopes of catching the dire hugag and freeing whoever was within its belly. Nineteen hugags fell that fateful week, each cut open to reveal only a collection of undigested tree barks, before one was found that, when slit, emitted a pale young woman, clad in a dress made from pine needles, clutching a human skeleton.

She explained quickly that she and her mother had been accidentally swallowed whole by a weak-eyed hugag when she was a mere babe, presumably while the two of them sat on the low-hanging branch of a pine tree. Unable to escape from the creature's stomach, the two had learned to adapt to life inside the hugag. They ate pine needles and bark, and the occasional passing snake. They kept themselves sane by humming hymns and reciting what few verses of Longfellow's "Evangeline" the mother could remember. Finally, the mother died from terminal despair and the young woman found herself alone, accompanied only by her mother's skeleton, which she used as an armchair.

She was very grateful to be freed at last from her strange captivity. She was especially happy to see the sun, about which she had heard many stories. And so the mystery of the talking hugag was solved.

"This kind of thing probably happens more often than we know," said the governor of Wisconsin, Robert M. La Follette, Sr., in his official statement to the media. The young woman's pine needle dress was donated to the Smithsonian.

And that young woman grew up to be my wife.

The hugag who could say "blart" and "grah" turned out also to be a fake.

Of course, the mother's skeleton was also donated to the Smithsonian, but it was later stolen and used as a xylophone.

Gumberoo

(Triskaidecapus elastica)

Unique among all animals, the gumberoo possesses thirteen limbs.

The gumberoo's forelimbs are long and gorilla-like, while its three hind legs are squat. Its remaining eight limbs radiate from around its abdomen, like the spokes of a wheel, permitting the fearsome creature to roll itself through the rain forests of Washington State and south to Oregon at speeds almost faster than the eye can see. Such a trip inevitably makes the creature dizzy, and so it never travels far in this fashion.

The gumberoo's rubbery skin is remarkable for its resiliency. Nothing seems to penetrate it. Clubs and axes rebound harmlessly with a rubber "boinging" sound, and bullets fired at the gumberoo inevitably sink in before bouncing back, directly at the rifle that fired it. In at least four cases (in 1816, twice in 1897, and in September 1903), the bullet has reentered the very rifle barrel it came from; but usually the return is slightly off, and the would-be hunter finds himself shot, quite rudely, with his own bullet.

Most have learned not to shoot at the gumberoo,

although in the gloaming the gumberoo can easily be mistaken for a bear wearing a belt of legs, a not uncommon sight in the Pacific Northwest, which explains the error.

The fearsome creature spends most of its life hibernating, often wedged into a narrow crevice or uncomfortable hole: Its pliant skin and cartilaginous bones permit it to deform its body into unusual and amusing shapes. When it wakes, it is inevitably ravenously hungry; it becomes one of the most dangerous forces in the temperate rain forests, swinging through the trees and eating every animal it sees, bones and all. It can eat an entire bull moose in about four hours; an average-size Sunday school picnic, picnickers included, would take scarcely two. Its body distends after the repast, like a Frenchman's, to fit more food; and ever it wants more.

The rubbery skin of the gumberoo has no pores, and so the creature cannot sweat. Consequently, it is in perpetual risk of overheating, a risk only exacerbated by the flammability of its flesh. Exposed to open flame, the gumberoo burns brightly for only a few seconds before being reduced to memories and ash. After a forest fire, rangers report a distinctive stench throughout the burnt-over regions, the stench of hundreds of hibernating gumberoo gone to glory.

It smells like a tire fire.

Of the innumerable attempts to take a gumberoo alive, the most celebrated was that of Gavrilo Princip, who spent ten months in 1913 and early 1914 hunting gumberoo.

Princip tried everything to trap the gumberoo. He dug pits, as we all, dear reader, have dug so many pits to capture fearsome creatures; but the gumberoo, upon falling in, simply bounced back out every time. He tried dropping cages and nets on the gumberoo, only to find its rubbery form easily slipped through the narrow bars and the tiny mesh. He sought the beast in winter, hoping that the cold would hinder its springy nature, so it could be knocked senseless by a club to the head. Unfortunately, in the cold the gumberoo grows brittle, and Princip only shattered his prey.

And all the time he hunted, Princip was in deadly danger, for the gumberoo possesses three methods of locomotion—strolling along the ground, swinging through the trees, and rolling like a wheel—and escape from a creature with three methods of locomotion is all but impossible. We have already mentioned the voracious appetite of the gumberoo.

"I'm not afraid," Princip told reporters.

At last Princip enlisted the aid of a mysterious species from Pennsylvania with the unfortunate name of "timberdoodle." (Other Pennsylvanian animals include the archaeothyris and the carbonerpeton.) The timberdoodle is a small carnivore unique in that once it bites down, its jaws will not open again until it hears the sound of thunder; during dry spells, the creature may well starve. Princip knew that in the rain forests of Washington, the timberdoodle would have no such troubles, and brought it thence in a sack. Princip then set to work tracking the gumberoo—the easiest part of his job, for few creatures in the wild lay tracks like a unicycle's.

Indeed, Princip soon found a gumberoo still slightly dizzy from its travels, and he sicced the timberdoodle on it. If most creatures were to bite a gumberoo, their jaws would bounce right back open, but, of course, the timberdoodle's jaws could not reopen in the absence of thunder, so it kept its grip on the rubbery flesh of the gumberoo.

The startled gumberoo took to the trees in a panic, rapidly swinging away through the low branches, leaving a long, distended, rubbery trail of stretched skin behind it. The rubbery trail grew longer and longer, as the timberdoodle (by this point Gavrilo had staked down the biter with croquet wickets) could not let go, and the gumberoo would not stop fleeing. Migrating deer passing south were caught in the stretching band, which bounced and flung them back, confused and cold, to the freezing north of British Columbia.

By this point, Princip (an excitable man) thought his game was all but caught, but unfortunately the sound of deer being catapulted backward so resembled thunder that the timberdoodle opened its jaws. Predictably, like a stone in a slingshot, the gumberoo was launched forward, and it flew through the air, out of sight. But midflight it struck a mountainside—probably Glacier Peak—and rebounded backward, eventually landing and rolling gently right toward an ecstatic Princip.

Here was the deadly scourge of the Northwest, unstoppable and hitherto uncatchable, stunned from its unprecedented journey.

"Nothing left to do but roll it to civilization," said Princip, smiling smugly to himself, moments before an ash from his cigarillo fell on the stunned gumberoo. The fearsome creature ignited, and an instant later there was nothing left of Princip's dreams but a fine spray of ash smudging his face. Brokenhearted, with only a timberdoodle in his sack, he returned to civilization, or at least to Olympia, Wash.

Once Princip reached the city, he began to sicken and weaken. He was short of breath. He had a hard time keeping food down. Doctors diagnosed him with tuberculosis, but they diagnosed everyone with tuberculosis in those days. Modern medicine was in its infancy; how were doctors to know that the incinerated gumberoo had coated 65 percent of Princip's internal organs with a rubbery film that hindered respiration and almost entirely prevented digestion? Food just bounced off his stomach and out his mouth again. It was disgusting—it was also killing him.

As his body consumed itself and he realized he did not have long to live, Princip abandoned his hunt for the gumberoo and vowed to bag the biggest game of all— he vowed, in the little time he had left, to hunt down the Archduke Ferdinand. Such an audacious and romantic hunt captured the imagination of the people of Olympia, and they all gathered around the train station, as he began his journey to Europe, to wish Princip good hunting. His eyes were sunken, his face sallow, and he looked like a dead man already; but such are the dooms and the dangers of hunting gumberoo.

And so the record remains: No one has ever captured a gumberoo alive, although Princip did catch his other prey, in the end.

So many stories in the lumberwoods are terrifying and sad that it's heartwarming to report that a man achieved his dream.

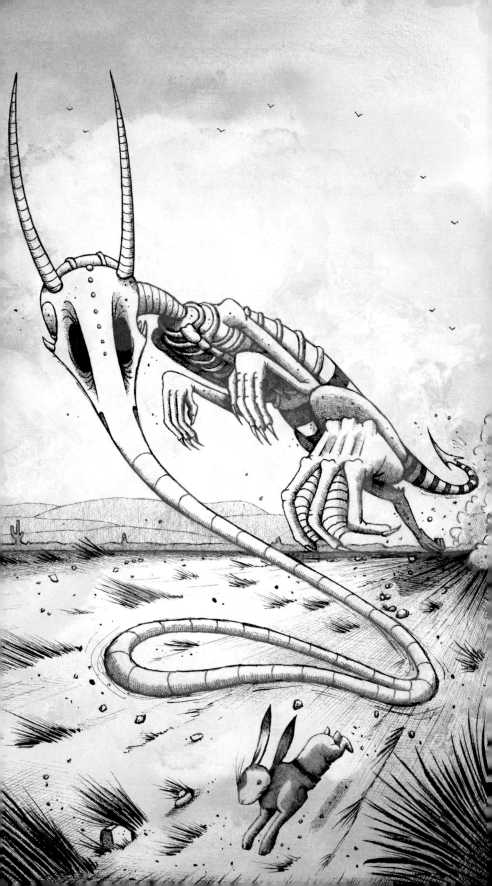

Roperite

(Malicius dominguesensis)

About thirty years ago I was searching for carnivorous butterflies in the American Southwest when I heard the word "roperite" spoken in hushed tones by a group of Paiute prospectors. They were referring to a local web-footed desert biped with a long, prehensile beak that ends in a lariat. "That doesn't sound so scary," I said to myself, "because I am not afraid of lariats."

Then my companions pointed out how close a lariat is to a noose.

Science says that when a male toad hatches a sow's egg under a gibbous moon, the result is a roperite. But the natives of the Mojave Desert tell a different tale. They speak of a time, two hundred years ago, when the desert land was fertile and choked with whipper weed, and the Spanish crown parceled it out into ranchos, on which herds of fat cattle roamed, grazing and causing mischief.

It was a cruel era, and the men who lived through it were bloodthirsty scallywags;

but the cruelest of all was the rancher known as José Maria Dominguez. Night and day he'd ride through the whipper weeds of his rancho looking for cattle rustlers to lasso and drag to their deaths, as was the custom at the time. He became so adept at the practice that cattle rustlers did not offer sufficient sport, and he began lassoing other creatures, too, such as vagabonds, drunks, jackrabbits, and orphans. It is likely that many of those he served so harshly did not deserve it, especially the orphans. But one does not win the title "cruelest of all" by handing out candy. To be fair to the man, he worked hard to achieve his dream. And when he died, the Paiute said, his spirit walked the land on two webbed feet, still lassoing the helpless and dragging them to their deaths.

Thus was he either rewarded for his hard work or punished for his cruelty, depending on your viewpoint. (The spirit of Dominguez's horse became a species of flowering cactus, which seems less apt. But the ways of the desert are strange.)

Whether the Paiute were correct about José Maria Dominguez, or just pulling my leg—not the wooden one, the fleshy one—the fact of the roperite is indisputable. We simply don't know if the creature is the specter of that old Mexican rancher or a natural creature that eats and breeds and spreads diseases.

Are there many roperites, or only one? Only one has ever been seen at a time, but this proves nothing; have you ever, dear reader, seen two unicorns at the same time? Some creatures are just antisocial, and an animal that murders anything it sees with its nooselike beak . . . I would call that antisocial.

No footage exists of a roperite attack, but eyewitness descriptions are particularly spine-chilling. Silently racing on its enormous webbed feet, the roperite comes speeding over the sands, faster than a cactus cat. Its serpentine beak with its curious loop lashes out and grabs you, or a nearby orphan. Lucky is the man who finds the roperite's lariat land around his throat, for he is soon strangled; the unlucky is dragged over the harsh and abrasive Mojave sands.

It all happens very quickly. He may think, "Aw, this isn't so bad," but then he looks down and sees that his legs have been half worn away and he is being dragged along on his quickly disappearing knees.

Mercifully, the victim is usually reduced to a few wisps of skin and hair before full realization sets in.

Horses cannot outrun it; mongooses cannot outrun it; dune buggies it passes on the left; roadrunners, says cryptzoologist William T. Cox, it "steps on or kicks out of the way."

One creature immune to the predations of the roperite is the shar-pei breed of dog. If you have ever seen a shar-pei, you will know that it is covered with loose, wrinkled skin. When a shar-pei is dragged by a roperite, its skin does not wear off, as yours would, dear reader; it just unspools, stretching further and further out behind it, as one by one the wrinkles disappear. Eventually the roperite tires, and releases its prey; the pup finds itself confused in the desert, with smooth, wrinkle-free skin and a long flesh trail behind it, which it can follow home.

Since the roperite is a purely malicious creature with no redeeming features, not even attractive plumage, locals have long put bounties on the beast. Those who have hunted it have all come to grief:

Some have been dragged to their doom when their erstwhile prey got the drop on them, but others have perished in a stranger manner.

Although it is possible to wound a roperite with a bullet, no one has as yet managed to kill one; and the roperite is so fast, it turns out, that even wounded it can whirl around in a half circle so that the bullet comes out the far side, heading right back at the hunter. Few who have wounded a roperite have lived to tell about it. And the injured creature lopes off into the desert to lick its wounds, recuperate, and await the chance to return.

There is only one man who is known to have thwarted the roperite unequivocally, and that is Hueco Slim.

Hueco Slim was a rough customer who rode the range at the turn of the last century until the encroaching trolley cars and telegraph poles scared him off for good. He was famous for his gruff demeanor, his epic stubble, and his wire-thin frame, the thinnest in the territories. His horse, a mare named Flaca, was even thinner, and most people found her peaked back too narrow to perch on and would just slip right off; but Hueco Slim's narrow buttocks sat on her bareback like a knife edge on a knife edge; and in this way they traveled the length and breadth of the Southwest.

Coming down through the Sierra Nevadas one morning, Hueco Slim saw the dread figure of the roperite bearing down on him. Although he put the spurs to Flaca, he knew that outrunning the creature was impossible, and sure enough, the roperite had soon caught up and threw its noose of a beak over

Hueco Slim. But Hueco Slim proved so slim that when the roperite drew its noose tight, Slim *turned sideways* and *passed right through it.*

Three times the creature lassoed Slim, and three times the cowboy turned sideways and escaped. Despairing, the roperite managed to lasso Slim's mare, but when it cinched its beak, one of Flaca's razor-sharp protruding ribs sliced the lariat in two. Hueco Slim and his mare rode away, leaving a useless, nooseless roperite behind them with a tear in its eye.

Either the roperite healed, or learned to splice, or there are more than one of them, because it has killed at least twice since then. The last recorded time was in 1993, when Lester Blemmelmann was snatched from a tour group, dragged and sanded away until nothing remained but his metal hip.

If you see a sow's egg, you might be tempted to destroy it, to help rid the world of this scourge; but I would request, dear reader, that you mail it to me instead. I have a plan to domesticate roperites and use them to haul novelty wagons through amusement parks, but I need some breeding stock. I will pay with blood diamonds or Confederate dollars. I can't see how this could go wrong.

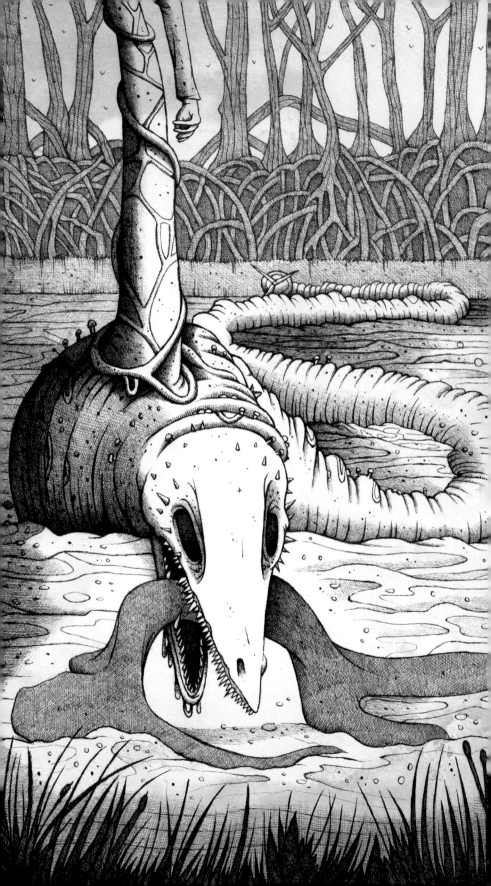

Snoligoster

(Rotorcaudus dorsocerus)

In the swamps of Florida, Georgia, and Louisiana, the alligators fear the bootleggers, and the bootleggers fear the alligators, and they both fear the snoligoster as they fear no other creature.

Although many animals will prey on humans—such as the puma, the tick, the Frenchman, and the hodag—only the snoligoster is cruel and vain enough to parade its victims around after slaying them.

The snoligoster has no limbs, but it does sport a large, curved horn sprouting from its back. When hunting, the creature seizes its prey in its powerful jaws and flips the poor sap backward, impaling him on the dorsal spike.

The effect is quite delightful to watch, but also tragic and disgusting; nevertheless, if you are at all interested in juggling or acrobatics, dear reader, or in the ball-and-cup game, it is worth your while to seek out and spy on a snoligoster on the hunt. With luck, you will see the creature impale an evil person, and then you won't have to feel so bad.

After mounting its prey on its horn, the snoligoster speeds through the swamps until it reaches a particularly sunny place, where it swims back and forth in the sunshine, as if displaying the impalee with pride. It does this because what the snoligoster eats is not flesh, but only the shadows of flesh, and only by hoisting that flesh high upon the spike can it bend its long neck to graze upon its victim's shadow.

Naturally, the creature does not hunt at night; nor does it hunt at noon, when the sun is high and casts no shadows. Morning and evening show the longest shadows, and therefore the most nourishing repast.

Sometimes the poor victim impaled upon the spike lingers, still alive and in such cases must bear the agony of being transfixed as well as the humiliation of having his shadow consumed.

In one memorable instance, Louisiana governor Huey Pierce Long, during a morning photo op in the bayou, sat on what he had assumed was a moss-covered log. It was not a log.

Moments later, he was tossed through the air and landed on the snoligoster's horn, which passed right through the region where his heart should have been (he kept his heart in an ivory box in the state capitol). As the snoligoster swam back and forth in the beautiful sunshine, Governor Long begged someone in the crowd to kill him and end his misery, but no one knew how, so instead everyone took pictures and shouted encouragement. The photographs, thanks to the snoligoster's tasteful sense of lighting, were extremely attractive, and when printed on nickel postcards sold quite well. The late governor is still known in Louisiana as "Huey Pierced Lung," and everyone has a good laugh.

Not all encounters with the beast end in such a jovial and amusing way, though. I once housed a young snoligoster in a swamp pen in my personal menagerie, cultivated and maintained by Hans, my manservant. Hans disobeyed my direct orders because they interfered with his cartoons, and tended to his maintenance duties—mostly raking and weeding—not at noon but as evening came. Needless to say, Hans's shadow fell through the chain-link fence, directly in the snoligoster's path. Hans appeared the next morning with only the ragged stump of a shadow, and it was weeks before a new one, thinner and wispier and a little off-center, grew in. This is the kind of tragedy that can befall one who is careless around a fearsome creature.

Most terrifying is the story of the snoligoster and Lawrence Alaminos, a man afflicted with that strange disease known as "biumbralism." After fooling around with forbidden experiments in the dark arts, Alaminos had accidentally acquired a second shadow that spread across the ground at right angles to his own.

This shadow craved human blood and would whisper to Alaminos, when it grew long and powerful, that he must serve it in the name of evil. Alaminos sought me out for advice, and, in my tasteful oak-paneled library, where candles projected the mocking, prancing form of Alaminos's evil shadow on the wall, I told him to seek out the snoligoster, for no other creature had the power to consume shadowstuff.

Alaminos caught the next bus to Florida. The passing streetlights shining through the Greyhound window set his shadows moving in crazy crisscross designs along the walls.

"At your touch the innocent must burn," one shadow cackled, in a voice only Alaminos could hear. The other shadow stayed mute. Alaminos brushed the sweat from his brow and offered a silent prayer that he would succeed in his mission or die in the swamps; already he could feel himself growing slightly mad.

Somewhere in the Okefenokee Swamp, among the mosquitoes thick as fog and leeches large as baguettes, Lawrence Alaminos must have found a snoligoster; he must have contrived to grapple with it and cling to its dorsal horn; he must have screamed as the fearsome creature swam to the sunny glade and tore out his shadow by the roots. He must have laughed with relief as he fled the swamps.

I ran into Alaminos several years later at one of the countess's parties. The pupils of his eyes were fully dilated, and he could not stop his maniacal grinning. He cast a single shadow, as all decent people do.

"I see you survived the snoligoster," I said, tipping my hat in congratulations.

Alaminos drew from his sleeve a curved dagger with a skull-head pommel. At that moment I realized what had happened.

The snoligoster had

eaten the wrong shadow.

Leprocaun

(Pygmailicius hibernicus)

The leprocaun is closely related to the more famous leprechaun, although it is poorer and less obsessed with marshmallows. Leprocauns are indigenous to Ireland and were introduced into Canada in the 1830s, when they stowed away on boats bringing Irish immigrants. (The Irish population of leprocauns was later exterminated—consumed, it is said, by hungry Irishmen. The last leprocaun in Ireland was seen in 1851; he was braised and served with a sprig of parsley.)

Leprocauns are noted for their skill at playing haunting melodies on pipes fashioned from cat-tails. Although they resemble leprechauns to some extent, they are uglier and more savage-looking.

They wear trousers made of rat skin and shoes made of hamster skulls. Whereas catching a leprechaun might get you a pot of gold, catching a leprocaun will get you nothing more than fleas, and perhaps a nasty rash.

Furthermore, in Canada, the leprocaun revealed a malicious side rarely displayed in its native land. While in Ireland, the leprocaun was content to play little tricks, perhaps stealing your key ring and replacing it with a ring of braided tapeworms. In Canada, the leprocaun's tricks were more nefarious—they began obsessively stealing the noses, and ears, off corpses, and replacing them with false noses, and ears, made of cheese.

As the leprocaun population grew throughout the late nineteenth century (for the nasty little vermin breed like rabbits) the number of corpses so mutilated grew to epidemic proportions. A town would know that a leprocaun had set up inside its borders because suddenly every wake would be spoiled by a mourner's shriek: A child would stretch out a hand to wish Grandma a final good-bye as she lay in her coffin and would accidentally knock off her nose; a nose that proved to be Muenster cheese. It soon became the custom throughout Canada to tweak the nose and tug the ears of a corpse before the coffin closed—just in case.

The leprocaun is very skilled at shaping cheese, and the noses and ears look very life-like on the dead. Where the leprocauns get the cheese is unknown; some say they make it themselves, between their hideous toes. What they do with the noses and ears they steal is well established: They eat them raw, calling it revenge for the massacres and extinction they suffered. They talk about this while chewing the noses and ears, showing the half-chewed organs in their vile little mouths, and spraying bits of cartilage everywhere.

They really are filthy little creatures.

Up-to-date funeral directors now equip their parlors with electrified screens, trained leprocaun-hunting scorpions, motion detectors, and false poison noses. But for a long time these modern contrivances were unavailable, and desperate people were forced to sit up all night with a beloved corpse before burial, a broom in hand, ready to beat off any encroaching leprocauns. For the leprocaun is small and bendy and can fit even through a mouse hole.

In Kitchener, Ontario, in 1935, one particularly malignant and cunning leprocaun proved the terror of the town. It had mastered a particular tune on its cattail pipes, a potent lullaby that drove all listeners to dreamtown. I mean they took a bite of the sleep sandwich. I mean that after three bars they were snoring.

Corpses in Kitchener got interred immediately; but this was not always practical, and often the body had to wait overnight for burial. And when it did, come morning, its ears and nose were cheese. Relatives wept. Town officials gnashed their teeth. But every time, whoever stayed up guarding the body woke the next morning next to a mutilated body, ashamed of his failure.

When the homecoming queen of 1936 choked on pep pills one Saturday night, the town council feared her attractive and popular face would be marred by cheese organs, so they put out a call for a doughty soul to stand guard until the cemetery opened on Sunday. Great rewards, key to the city, the hand of the mayor's daughter: They offered the works. And one who heard was a young man just drifted into town. He was headed westward to Regina by broken-down train and had to spend the night in Kitchener anyway while they adjusted the railway gauges; why not volunteer to guard the body? He brought a thermos of coffee and a thermos of Kenyan dust tea, the strongest tea there is; he had a broom and a pack of chewing gum. Hopeful townsfolk locked him in the funeral home, in a small room with an open coffin.

"If the leprocaun get from her face," they warned him, in broken English, for they mainly spoke Kitchenerese, "it will be the harm for you."

The young man paced the floor of the room, swigging from his thermos and furiously chewing gum. He could see through a small barred window the lights of the town wink out one by one. An old-fashioned clock on the wall, the kind with Roman numerals, ticked the slow seconds by. A single bulb cast long, strange shadows on the walls. And there in the room with him was the corpse of the young woman.

He would neither sleep nor, the young man told himself, go mad.

As the clock outside tolled two, strange, soft music began to play. The young man found his eyelids growing heavy . . .

But, realizing that this must be the leprocaun, he slapped himself in the face. He ran a few laps around the small room. Soon the music stopped and he could resume his vigil.

An hour or so later the music started again. By this time the coffee was gone, and he was afraid that if he drank any more tea he'd need to slip away to the bathroom, leaving the corpse unguarded. He slammed the coffin lid on his fingers a few times and kept himself awake until the ominous tune stopped.

By this time it was the darkest, strangest time of night. The young man's feet ached from the hours spent pacing the room. The rush from the coffee was wearing off. His fingers hurt, too. The corpse had shifted position when he'd slammed the coffin lid, and now, with the lid back open, he could see the head cocked to one side, as though listening.

But there was nothing to listen to except the horrible ticking of the clock.

Just to make sure the corpse was still whole, he reached into the coffin and pinched the girl's nose. It was real, but it was cold as ice, and the strange, rubbery sensation of a dead face filled him with disgust and dread. He was no longer so sure he could hold out for a full night. "We're going to make it," he said to her, although he did not believe it. Then he said, "Green church-mouse ire box." Only in the smallest and tiredest hours of the morning can the world seem so confusing.

It was just before the dawn that he heard the pipes again. He covered his ears and thrashed about to stay conscious. As he staggered about the room, he was only dimly aware of the things he was knocking over: a hat rack, an umbrella stand, some filing cabinets, and, finally, with a tremendous crash, the coffin. Screaming from fear and agony he fell down over the mess and lost consciousness.

He could not have been asleep long, and he awoke to the sound of the door unlocking. Quickly standing up, he was soon surrounded by concerned townsfolk, wondering at the disorder of the room. But although the queen's carcass had unceremoniously been spilled out on the ground, her ears and nose were quite real. The leprocaun had been kept at bay!

There was a hearty cheer, and the young man found himself an instant celebrity. The town hoisted him on their shoulders and paraded him about. His reward, measured out in gold bullion, began to pile up in the town square. By the time everything was toted up, the sun was beginning to climb toward noon. The young man felt a trickle, as of sweat, on his neck. Reaching up (between congratulatory handshakes) to brush it aside, he touched his earlobe, which separated in a goopy mess. The adoring crowd set their autograph books down and stared in horror. The young man's ears and nose were nothing but cheese, cheese that under the warmth of the sun had begun to melt. The leprocuan had done its grisly work.

The young man slunk away into the strange places and the mysteries. And you must know, dear reader, *that young man was I*.

I was able to parlay my reward into the beginnings of the fortune that funded many of my expeditions. And I did claim the hand of the mayor's daughter; it was mechanical, and made of aluminium.

Let us never speak of this again.

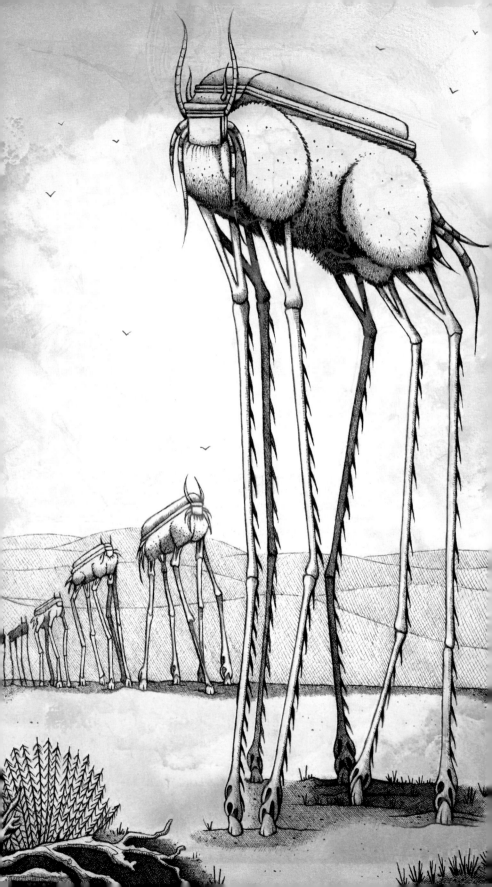

Funeral Mountain Terrashot

(Morgellons explosissimus)

One of the strangest and most haunting sights offered to travelers in the Amargosa Desert is the procession of the terrashot. A long, single-file line of the wobbly, unsteady creatures comes winding down from the Funeral Mountains into the heat of the desert and their ultimate doom.

The terrashot is an odd creature, part animal and part fungus, in much the same way that a lichen is part fungus and part alga, or a cockatrice is part rooster and part serpent. It grazes in meadows in the Funeral Mountain heights, romping on three to seven legs, until some mysterious instinct drives whole herds of them into the desert.

Long part of Native American oral tradition, this procession was first recorded in 1846 by members of the Mormon Battalion under Lt. Col. Philip St. George Cooke. The lieutenant colonel noted the incident in his diary, in the curiously concise code employed by the U.S. Army at the time; "⟨◫⋔Ⴠ⟩⊶⊖⤬▷" he wrote, which decodes as: "We are done for! An uncanny procession of living caskets we have witnessed march into the desert! Lucky is the man who has died ere this day, as assuredly fell doom awaits us."

For the creatures did indeed resemble coffins—coffins with unsteady legs. A more sober assessment came from Private Orson Schultz, who rode close enough to the creatures to describe them in detail in a letter he sent to his beloved mother. He noted that the terrashot (as they were later known) all measured six to eight feet in length, with rectangular, oblong bodies. The back of the terrashot, as Schultz noted, is covered with a hard carapace, like the polished wood of a casket.

Along its sides and underbelly, however, the creature is soft to the touch, "like a moth's ears," Schultz wrote. Schultz was also the first to describe the strange fate of the terrashot. As the terrashot herd ambled single file into the desert, Schultz watched the heat of the sun swell each terrashot, until finally they would explode with a terrific report.

Schultz did not have the biological knowledge we do now, so he did not understand that the terrashot's apparently suicidal trek is really its method of reproduction: When the wind from the desert is blowing toward the mountains, the creature arranges for the desert heat to explode it and scatter its spores, which are wind-borne back to the mountains. Frankly, what happens next science is not too sure of, but whatever it is,

a new generation of terrashot springs up to wander, in turn, into the desert when the wind is right.

The terrashot's explosion in the desert, which is powerful enough to leave a crater in the sand, is one of the loudest macroevents in nature, surpassed only by the rut-roaring of the sphinx and the daily screaming of the earthworms (which happens at a frequency too high for humans to hear, fortunately). "I am blest I was not closer," Orson Schultz wrote his mom, "for I should have certainly been reduced to my component atoms from the force of the event."

Schultz, a versatile observer, also recorded

in the highlands of Missouri an early sighting of the jimplicute, a vampiric sauropod. I acquired a bundle of his correspondence in an estate sale in the late '50s, and I have taken his sage advice to heart: Never have I dared approach a terrashot in the desert too closely, lest I perish when it does.

Not everyone has been as circumspect, though. Witness the sad case of Gloria Grundy and Scaraband Thompson-Chang of Glenvale, Nevada. These two lovebirds had been picnicking in the highlands when the procession of the Funeral Mountain terrashot swayed by. Unwisely they pursued the creatures into the desert, unaware that they could prove fearsome.

When the first terrashot exploded, Mr. Thompson-Chang, who was trying to ride the fool thing, was turned to dust, more or less. Miss Grundy was far enough away from the blast that she only suffered a ruptured eardrum, but she was, tragically, downwind, which meant she inhaled a vast quantity of terrashot spores (as well as, presumably, much of the remaining mass of her late boyfriend). She returned to Glenvale in mourning, and the police filed her report under *creatures, fearsome*—a catchall for the mysterious and unsolvable. Gloria Grundy seemed a little ill, but this was dismissed as nerves. At dinner with her parents she foamed at the mouth a little. One day later, concerned friends noticed a fine down was sprouting from her skin.

"It's just nerves," she said, somewhat mechanically.

She died that night, peacefully in her bed. What was most remarkable was that she was found with the covers kicked to the floor, lying in a coffin as though in state. The mysterious coffin, with its fuzzy sides and shiny lid, would be her final resting place. The coroner noted, in a report that he filed too late, that the coffin appeared to have *sprouted from her body*.

As soon as I heard about this curious incident through my contacts in the Bureau, I sent a telegram posthaste to the

officials in Glenvale, Nevada, warning them. I had to send it collect, though, and it is possible they never received it. Gloria Grundy's last wish was to be cremated, and friends and family, including the surviving members of the Thompson-Chang clan, were gathered in the Glenvale Funeral home. OPEN 24 HOURS / WE NEVER CLOSE read the sign on the door. SIC TRANSIT GLORIA GRUNDY read the message on the funerary wreath. Everyone clustered around as the casket trundled down the conveyer belt toward the crematorium. The heat was getting oppressive. The casket began to swell. Everyone took a deep breath . . .

Stay out of Glenvale, dear reader, is what I'm saying. You don't want to go there.

Slide-Rock Bolter

(Leviathanella mucopuruluntius)

The slide-rock bolter is so reclusive and mysterious that its existence was unknown in 1919, when Giuseppe Zangara Orifice, a postwar immigrant from Austria-Hungary, purchased a large and fertile valley in Colorado with the money he had made profiteering. Giuseppe Zangara Orifice intended to raise sheep, as was the custom at the time, but twice he awoke in the morning to find that a good half of his flock had disappeared in the night, the fence to their pen shattered and flattened. Two halves, disappeared twice, means no flock left, as simple arithmetic will teach us.

Thoroughly confused, but despairing of raising disappearing sheep, Giuseppe Zangara

Orifice rented his valley out as a sanatorium for rich people with tuberculosis. One night an entire bungalow, with sixteen consumptives inside, disappeared.

The survivors coughed up terrible stories of a strange rumbling sound at night.

What neither Giuseppe Zangara Orifice nor the sanatorium director knew, but what you, dear reader, have probably guessed, was that both sheep and consumptives had been swallowed whole by an enormous land fish known to posterity as the slide-rock bolter.

This bolter, it turned out, hung from the summits of nearby mountains by its hooked caudal fin, exuding from innumerable disgusting pores a mucopurulent secretion. At night it would release itself with a flick of the tail and skid down the mountainside, the lubricating mucopurulence protecting its soft underbelly. Zipping through the valley with its wide mouth open, it swallowed whole whatever man, beast, plant, or structure was in its path. Momentum and a little judicious wriggling would carry it to the top of the next mountain, where it would hook its tail and rest, digesting. The slimy trail it left behind evaporated in the dawn. So high was its perch, swaddled in clouds and concealed by crevices and trees, that none knew or suspected that an enormous fish had been responsible for all the damage and havoc. But they knew something was wrong.

The sanatorium closed down, and Giuseppe Zangara Orifice rented the remaining buildings out to an orphanage, which was less fussy about safety.

Seventy-seven orphans were guzzled by the bolter over the course of one dread week.

People were frantic. Was the valley haunted? "Of course it is not haunted," I would have told them if they had asked me, and if I had been alive a hundred years ago and had also possessed the power of fore-sight. "It is simply the hunting ground of an enormous land fish." People can be so superstitious and silly sometimes.

Now, there are many well-authenticated stories of people swallowed by great fish or whales and surviving—Jonah, Ruggiero, and Geppetto are three examples—so you may hope that a thriving community of orphans, consumptives, and sheep will eventually be found in the bolter's belly. Unfortunately, a bolter's esophagus passes through three giz-zards lined with razor-sharp chitinous teeth. So no orphans, et al., will ever be found inside the bolter; but many pieces of orphans will be.

No one dared live in Giuseppe Zangara Orifice's accursed valley, because of cowardice and the 80 percent fatality rate. Short on funds and almost in despair, Giuseppe Zangara Orifice gave a discount rate to a leper colony. The lepers were unenthused with the location. One raised his fist in protest, but it fell off, and the rest sat docilely around the valley, awaiting their fate. Did they pray to their leper gods? Did they weep leprous tears?

That night there was a tremendous crashing sound, as there so often was, and a whole cottage and its twelve leprous inhabitants were found missing. But this proved to be the end of the bolter's reign of terror.

Lepers are delicious, but they are also contagious. In the process of digestion, the bolter contracted the disease. Leprosy is a grisly business, and all the more so in a fish the size of a railroad car.

Chunks of flesh sloughed off the bolter, tumbling downhill into the horrified valley. Eventually, the bolter tried to coast down through the valley one last time, but the rough ride was too much for its diseased body, which shivered to pieces at the bottom.

Giuseppe Zangara Orifice was delighted to find that the scourge of his valley was dead.

"A happy ending!" he crowed, forgetting the long queue of the dead among his tenants. With the money he had made massaging insurance claims and selling the bolter's body to science, he brought his family from the newly minted Kingdom of Serbs, Croats and Slovenes to his Colorado vale, and all twenty-six of them lived there in harmony among the pleasant greenery. "A happy ending." He chuckled to himself again.

Tragically, as is so often the case, it turned out that only the presence of an alpha-predator like the slide-rock bolter had kept the populations of other animals in check. With no bolter to scare them away, wolves, spider-wolves, overwolves, Frenchmen, and even a renegade hodag began to fill the valley. They ate the miserable Orifices one by one, starting with the youngest.

"Slide-rock bolter, please come back," shouted a weeping Giuseppe Zangara Orifice as the overwolves closed in on him. It was the last thing he ever said.

Toteroad Shagamaw

(Peripeteia garbagophagus)

The most fearsome creature of all, dear reader, is unpreparedness. It is for this reason that I award the toteroad shagamaw *second place*.

For I have sought two-headed snakes in Africa, feral koalas in Australia, behemoths in Asia, and Frenchmen in Europe; each has been deadly, but in each case I was prepared. However, the toteroad shagamaw is deceptive. The toteroad shagamaw plays a deep game.

In the lumberwoods of Maine and up into New Brunswick and Quebec, the shagamaw can be found scavenging along the outskirts of trailer parks and lumber camps. It will eat anything and everything, *including a man's right hand*, but it usually restricts itself to garbage and unattended pets. A "toteroad" is an old term for an access road that leads to a camp, and there's always plenty to eat along a toteroad, especially if you eat garbage.

The shagamaw's visage is fearsome, with a goat's features on a man's skull; about the mass and volume of a Jersey cow, but its feet are what are truly monstrous.

I have the honor of being the first to describe accurately and scientifically the toteroad shagamaw. I encountered it while seeking another creature: the legendary bear-foot boy. I had come across a set of bear tracks outside the town of Arrowsic, Maine, and I was following them in pursuit of the boy. There was always the chance that I might be stalking a real bear, of course, in which case I was ready. I had my bear-proof suit and my bear spray and a harpoon gun. No bear would get the jump on me.

For three miles I followed the trail before I realized that I had things all wrong; the trail I'd been following was not a trail of bear tracks after all; these were moose tracks.

I was embarrassed at having made such an elementary blunder as to mistake hooves for claws. Furthermore, to be on the track of a creature as fearsome as a moose when I was prepared for a bear, well, it was a dangerous situation.

Returning to camp, I swapped my bear-proof suit for a moose-proof suit, packed up some moose spray, and attached a new harpoon to my harpoon gun. I set off into the woods again and picked up the trail where I'd left it. I followed the moose tracks, feeling secure in my certainty that I was ready for any moose I might stumble across.

Three miles in I realized that I was right the first time: These were bear tracks. I rubbed my eyes, or at least the one remaining to me. "Has the world gone mad . . . or have I?" I whispered to myself.

Back at camp once more, I quickly changed into my bear-proof suit. I took the bear spray, and the vorpal bear harpoon, although just to be safe I brought the moose spray and the extra harpoon, too. If bear or moose were out there, I would be ready. (I had already forgotten all about the bear-foot boy, which is fairly typical of my attention span. Perhaps the bear-foot boy is just a myth; or perhaps I misheard something.)

I followed those bear tracks all day, and was horrified to find them change from a bear to a moose and from a moose to a bear. "Perhaps," I said to myself, "this is a moose who transforms into a bear when the moon is full, or every three miles or so." I was ready, however, for a weremoosebear. At least I thought I was ready.

Dear reader, the secret of the toteroad shagamaw is terrible to reveal. It has the forefeet of a bear; it has the hindfeet of a moose. It walks upright, as we do, and when its moose feet begin to tire, it pivots around its hips and walks on its forefeet, like a man walking on his hands.

Thus does the shagamaw surpise its prey! In 1987, Richard Hempelweiss thought he was hunting moose; the shagamaw ate him. In 1961, Constance Jackson thought she was on the trail of the bear that had stolen her honey jar collection; the shagamaw ate her. Preparing to fight a bear and a moose at the same time is next to impossible, and anyone preparing to fight both a bear and a moose will never be able to prepare simultaneously to fight a shagamaw. Witnessing the shagamaw switch from one set of feet to the other is a strangely disconcerting experience. Weaker minds have been driven mad by the sight. Indeed, when I finally caught up with the shagamaw, and there in a clearing I watched its transformation, I came close to passing out.

In an instant, the beast was upon me, and tore my right hand out by the root.

Confused, unprepared, very nearly literally disarmed, I must have appeared easy pickings for the vicious toteroad shagamaw. How overconfidently it danced around me on alternating pairs of feet!

But I possessed two things the shagamaw did not expect. One was a spare mechanical hand, which I had acquired from the daughter of the mayor of Kitchener, to attach to my bleeding stump. The other was a set of items I carried concealed behind my hunting gear: a rod and reel, a box of fishing tackle, and a bucket hat with hooks and lures threaded through it.

The shagamaw had come prepared to murder and consume a hunter. But it could not have foreseen that I was not just a hunter *but also a fly fisherman.*

I escaped to hunt, and fish, again another day. For the shagamaw was unprepared.

Wapaloosie

(Adorabilis arborealis)

Harmless and adorable, the wapaloosie scarcely appears deserving of the name "fearsome creature." And yet this little rodent is indirectly responsible for the Hoquiam massacre of 1993, the worst disaster in the history of the state of Washington since the injuring of Gavrilo Princip.

The wapaloosie feeds exclusively on the "canopy fungus" that grows at or near the tops of the trees in its native habitat in the Pacific Northwest. A spike at the end of its tail helps anchor the Wapaloosie during a particularly precarious climb. But few climbs are precarious for this creature, as there is no more skilled or fanatical climber in the animal kingdom. It lives a completely arboreal existence and knows no joy other than ascending trees in search of the fungus that makes up its diet.

"Even a monkey falls out of a tree sometimes," sages say; but the wapaloosie never.

One October, in 1993, local entrepreneur Martina Kasprowicz found a wapaloosie feeding high in her backyard. Kasprowicz felt protective of canopy fungi, due to an old but unforgotten schoolgirl crush; with bird shot she gunned the wapaloosie down.

Not wanting to let its carcass go to waste, but well aware that wapaloosie flesh is too sour to eat, Kasprowicz, on a whim, skinned it. Its hide was velvety and soft, and she had one of the local taxidermist-tailors fashion it into a pair of gloves.

You may not know much about the history and fashion of gloves, but refined persons always have a pair on hand, ready to slap boorish passersby in the face and call them to a duel. Kasprowicz's gloves were of such high quality that she could have challenged the King of Denmark to a duel, or the monarch of any other country of equal or lesser size. They were also warm, and waterproof. Their only drawback, she noted, was that she couldn't wear them hunting, as they were too thick to fit in her shotgun's trigger guard.

Kasprowicz was, as I have said, an entrepreneur, and she smelled a profit. One crisp October afternoon she headed out into the nearby lumberwoods, a shotgun cradled in her arm. Before evening fell, Kasprowicz had scored a sackful of wapaloosim (the correct plural). Making gloves from the creatures' skins required more technical skill than Kasprowicz possessed, but she was able to skin the wapaloosim and fashion their skins into simple scarves, which she took to the church bazaar that weekend.

Seventy-three scarves she brought to the bazaar, and seventy-three scarves she sold in the first few hours. The entire Hoquiam chapter of the Birdwatcher's Fellowship Society found them so enticing they adopted the scarf as part of their official uniform. roson bought two: one for himself bring to his sweetheart. Monica m said she would wear hers proudly ed the afternoon nature walk.

the simple townsfolk, preening hew scarves, went off with Monica Greenbaum to admire the foliage, Kasprowicz headed home and busied herself around the house. Donning her gloves, she went outside to rake leaves, but no sooner did she

take a rake in hand than something startling happened. As the gloves touched the wood handle, they leaped off Martina Kasprowicz's hands and scampered up the shaft. She tried touching the gloves to an ax handle, a wooden chair, and finally to a tall fir tree: Each time the gloves would wriggle and inch their way up the wood. At the final test they disappeared up the side of the tree, climbing their way into the high red leaves. Kasprowicz was utterly charmed. She wondered if the scarves she had sold would work the same way. And then a shadow passed over her face.

It was just a suspicion, but she drove back to the woods beside the church. She called out, softly at first, for the Birdwatcher's

Fellowship Society. She called out for the kind neighbors who had bought her scarves. She followed the trail of the nature walkers, and perhaps she felt a little sick with worry or anticipation. Only a slight echo answered her call, a slight echo and the distant sound of creaking.

The first person she caught up with was, predictably enough, Stumpy Monaserro. He was hanging from a tree, still wearing his wapaloosie scarf tied tight around his neck. One end of the scarf was still trying to inch its way up the tree, though Stumpy's weight kept it from making much progress. The efforts of his scarf had hanged him as surely as a thief at the gallows. His body swung back and forth, creaking. A few steps more and Kasprowicz saw the whole lot of them,

strangled, dangling from the trees like Christmas ornaments,

their scarves vainly attempting to ascend the trunks. The lighter among them were high up and almost out of sight, the heavier barely off the ground. Forty-three people, including the entire Hoquiam chapter of the Birdwatcher's Fellowship Society, died in those woods. Seven more of the seventy-three were hanged that day in separate incidents before word got around.

Cactus Cat

(Wampus bibulus)

The cactus cat belongs to the genus of animals known as wampus cats. It is said that all wampus cats are originally descended from beavers. A beaver was once cornered (scientists say) by a hungry wolverine, and there was nothing left for the beaver to do but climb a tree. But beavers cannot climb trees. Therefore, the beaver became a wampus cat, a wild feline with a ball at the end of its tail.

Wampus cats later evolved in different ways to suit their native habitat. The cactus cat, of course, has adapted to the deserts of the American Southwest, where its spiny body blends in with the local cacti.

The name Carlos Gutierrez will forever be linked with that of the cactus cat, for it is he who discovered, in 1852, the secret of why the cactus cat screeches at night. Wandering through the desert at night in search of moon shadows, Gutierrez saw a cactus cat slashing a cactus tree with its long claws, as the creature was known to do; but it did not drink the sap that oozed out of the gashes. Instead, it left the cactus flowing. Under the bright moonlight the cat's tracks were easily visible in the sand, so Gutierrez had no difficulty following as the cat went to cactus after cactus, *slashing* each one in turn and letting the sap run.

Eventually, the cat reached a cactus that had already been slashed. The sap that flowed from the gashes had thickened, like syrup, and clung to the cactus's spines. Gutierrez watched as the cactus cat approached the plant and licked up its thick, congealed ichor. After greedily lapping up every bit, the cat began to tremble. The needles that coated the cactus cat's body stood erect. The creature rolled back and forth in the sand before leaping up and issuing forth a scream so terrifying Gutierrez's hat flew off.

The cat screamed and ran in circles, finally racing over the horizon. "I am curious," said Gutierrez, "to learn what that substance is."

With the eye of science, we can now see that the sap, left for weeks to dry in the New Mexico sun, ferments into something part catnip and part feline mescal—that strong, maddening liquor of the Mexican borderlands. The cactus cat travels in a great circle, slashing some cactus trees to prepare them, while lapping up the fermented sap from others. The cactus cat is a territorial creature, and each one has its own rounds. Each one screams in the night.

The sap has no such effect on humans, any more than catnip does. But what every human must concede is that it tastes good on pancakes—an admirable substitute for maple syrup, which was hard to get in New Mexico Territory. Gutierrez discovered this and began slipping into the desert by day, and collecting the running sap before the noturnal cactus cat could awaken and come back for it. Gutierrez's Patented Flapjack Syrup and Vitality Tonic (as he called it) became a local sensation.

But the cat was not pleased. It could follow Gutierrez's tracks as easily as Gutierrez had followed its own, and it well knew that a man was pilfering its cactus sap. In the evening hours, the cat skulked on the edges of town.

Rarely had a cactus cat come this close to civilization, or to what passed for civilization in New Mexico Territory in 1852, and the townsfolk became worried. They said it seemed to be looking at people's boots as they passed by, as though seeking a particular pair. A pair that it recognized from the tracks around its cactus trees.

Gutierrez was too busy counting his money to know he was in danger. Early one morning as he strolled around the outskirts of the desert, dreaming of an empire based on syrup substitutes, the cactus cat flashed by. Its spiky tail, with the spiky ball on the end, whirled around Gutierrez so quickly that he barely registered it. The cat flew off into the desert, and Gutierrez, a little unnerved, hastened back into town. He stopped at his favorite saloon and, as he so often did of late, ordered a shortstack of pancakes, with plenty of Gutierrez's Patented Flapjack Syrup and Vitality Tonic.

It was not until he began drinking his orange juice that he noticed something was wrong: The orange juice was passing right through his body and staining his shirt. Gutierrez ripped open his shirt and found that his abdomen was riddled with a thousand tiny holes. The orange juice seeped right through them, dribbling along his belly. As he gasped in amazement, the juice squirted out with sudden force, like a sprinkler. Only then did Gutierrez realize what the cat had done to him with its terrible tail.

By the time he hit the floor he was already dead.

For the cactus cats, the damage had been done, though. As word got around that congealed sap from their cactus trees was the secret ingredient in Gutierrez's syrup, more and more people began tapping cactus trees. And so the cactus cat was driven further and further into the desert, where the cactus trees still grow succulent and tall. There in the wilderness, you can still hear them scream.

Squonk

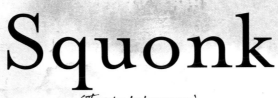

(Theristes lachrymosus)

In the wilds of the Pocono Mountains of Pennsylvania lurks the squonk. Its wrinkly skin is covered in warts and hangs from its body like a badly tailored suit. Its face, shaped like a rat's hindquarters with a pig's nose, is covered in warts. And its rheumy eyes weep constant tears.

It has yellowing, crooked tusks, but its most fearsome aspect is its misery. Most misery could scarcely be called fearsome, but the misery of the squonk is contagious.

The squonk is one of the last animals to evade capture. Hunting squonk does not sound difficult in theory, for the puddles of tears it leaves behind mark its trail. But in practice, to chase the squonk is impossible. As it scurries, trees and bushes bend aside to avoid contact with its hideous, warty skin, only to snap back after it passes. The hunter will never get close enough to get off a decent shot.

I sought the squonk myself, in the summer of '97. My sometimes nemesis and sometimes rival Jean-Paul Wentling had vowed to be the first to catch a squonk, and I had vowed to bag one before him. We pretended it was a friendly genteel rivalry, but I hated Wentling with all my shriveled Jarvik heart, and I would have murdered him gladly if not for the provisions of state and federal law.

Wentling and I had both been nominated for the Nobel Prize in cryptozoology after the war. You will notice I possess no Nobel Prize. We had both fallen in love with the Queen of Bakuba. You will perceive that "Prince of Bakuba" has never been among my innumerable titles. In short, Wentling had defeated me at every turn, and I swore an oath by my one good eye and by this mummified hand of St. Maximus the Confessor that this time I would get the best of him.

The grave, they say, has never turned its back on an opponent; instead, we all turn our backs on the grave. Well, I vowed never to turn my back on Wentling. I wasn't even sure what that meant, but my dander was up, and I may have been speaking in tongues. I really hated him.

But Wentling was a clever opponent, and while I built snares (that refused to come in contact with the squonk's nasty feet) and dug pits (that simply spat out again any squonks that fell in), Wentling had found himself a ratty old burlap sack, too old and ragged to care if it touched squonkmeat. He filled the sack with a baby's cries, with the sloshing of drowning kittens, and with the crashing of the 1929 stock market. Armed with nothing else, he sought the squonk.

It took him weeks of rooting through mud and burrfields, but Wentling finally worked his way close enough to a squonk that its gnarled cauliflower ears, clogged with wax and hair, could nevertheless make out the sounds rattling around inside that sack. Misery loves company, and to a squonk these sounds were irresistible. Wentling opened the sack, letting the carefully collected calliope of sound escape, and the squonk ran in. When he sealed the bag with a twist, the only sound was the sound of the squonk weeping.

It wept because it had been caught, of course; but it also wept because it was aware of its own hideousness and abjection. It wept because it would never know love (squonk breed through binary fission). It wept because its culture was inane and because someday it would die.

My hat is off to Wentling here; it was cleverly done. But Wentling being Wentling, he could not accept the victory with good graces. Still covered with filth and forest goo, he hastened to my large but unpretentious estate. I had only recently returned from a hard, futile day of squonk hunting, and the last thing I wanted was to hear the triumphant crowing of my deadliest rival, but, being a gentleman after a fashion, I saw Wentling into my study. There, beneath trophies of luckier hunts—the mounted Sasquatch head; the sciopod sock; the sealed opaque container that holds a basilisk eye—I met a smirking Jean-Paul Wentling.

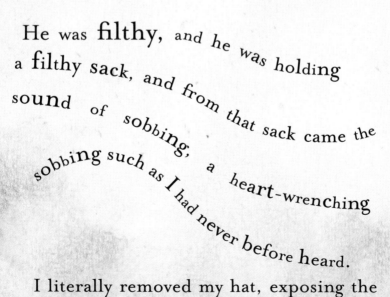

He was filthy, and he was holding a filthy sack, and from that sack came the sound of sobbing, a heart-wrenching sobbing such as I had never before heard.

I literally removed my hat, exposing the

metal plate over which hair no longer grows. Wentling was due that much.

"Perhaps you have noticed," that insufferable little prig said, "that I have hear a bag with a squonk in it." You will notice that he said *hear* instead of *here*; Wentling never had learned how to spell.

And in his subliterate, poorly spelled patois, he began to lecture me on his cunning victory; on his cleverness; on his innate superiority to your humble narrator. And the whole time the keening in the sack grew in volume, such that Wentling had to speak louder to be heard. Just as he had reached the climax of his irritating lecture, the weeping from the bag abruptly stopped.

Wentling and I stood in the eerie silence, eyeing each other across my desk carved from a leviathan's bacula.

With reluctant hands, Wentling opened his sack and looked inside.

Inside was only liquid.

The poor squonk had become so miserable that it dissolved in its own tears. There was nothing left of the squonk. There was no evidence that the squonk had ever been caught at all.

Wentling completely lost it at that point. His glory at being the first person to have ever caught a squonk melted away. "You'll tell them," he begged me, grabbing me by my smoking jacket, "you'll tell them I really did catch it." But, of course, I had never even seen the squonk, only heard what may have been one.

Weeping now, Wentling fell to his knees. "What's the use?" he said, again and again. And then he began to confess to me things no human being should know. His life was a failure. His wife was in love with her grand vizier. Sometimes, in the bathroom, he produced horrible things. Other times, he felt like he needed to sneeze, but no sneeze would come. He went on and on.

Now, I hated Wentling as few men have ever hated, but I could not bear to see a fellow creature in such paroxysms of despair. I sat him down in an armchair and went off to get him some Darjeeling tea with bergamot, a cup that always cheers. When I returned a few minutes later, the chair was empty. His clothes, soaking wet, were hanging off the chair. The chair was also soaking wet. Wet with tears.

There was nothing else left of Jean-Paul Wentling.

For the misery of the squonk is contagious misery. With fireplace tongs I carried his

88

sack outside, and I poured the squonk's tears down a storm drain. I burned Wentling's clothes, and I even burned the soaking arm-chair, even though it was a Louis XVI–style bergère, comfortable and hard to come by. I wasn't taking any chances.

No longer do I hunt Squonk.

Whirling Whimpus

(Vertex sp.)

In the upper peninsula of Michigan, there lives a creature called a dungavenhooter, which resembles a crocodile with no mouth. It pounds its prey with its heavy tail until the poor victim is reduced entirely to a gaseous form, which the dungavenhooter then inhales through its enormous nostrils. All its sustenance comes this way, through the nose, like the Astomi in India.

I mention the dungavenhooter because the power of its tail to reduce a moose calf or a hiker to gas is unprecedented in nature; but the power of the whirling whimpus comes close. While the dungavenhooter requires time and multiple blows to gasify its prey, the whimpus can, in an instant, reduce a grown man to a consistency that is usually described as "syrup." Being turned into syrup is not quite as bad as being turned into gas, dear reader, but it cannot be a pleasant experience.

The skill of the whimpus lies in its ability to spin at such a rapid velocity that it is almost invisible, resembling in this way the whirlwind that can only be detected by the pieces of leaf and dust swirling within. When the whimpus reaches its fastest rate of spin, it simply extends its long arms, and anything it touches instantly becomes syrup. Some call it slime or goo, but that is hardly appetizing. The greedy way the whimpus licks the stuff off its paws indicates that it must be syrup.

A whimpus usually feeds on deer and feral hogs, which abound in the Cumberland Mountains of Tennessee where it lives, but it will eat a human should one come across its path. Often these poor saps are declared missing, and, because search parties rarely look for syrup stains in their investigations, no trace of them is ever found. To call them lost is just wishful thing, as few are ever *lost* in the Cumberlands;

they are merely the food of the whimpus.

You may have heard of Troop 2—5 of the paramilitary youth militia known as the Boy Scouts of America. Today Troop 2—5 is famous for being a ragtag band of mystery-solving boy sleuths, but back in the dark days of 1978, the troop was known for a camping trip that ended in tragedy: the loss of six scouts, most of whose bodies were never recovered. Five of these scouts were tenderfoots, and hardly missed, but the sixth, Beauregard Shagtemple, had earned the coveted merit badge in phrenology, and so search parties combed the area for weeks—to no avail.

Beauregard Shagtemple was my nephew, and the young scamp had hidden the keys to my strongbox a week before disappearing, so it was particularly important to me that he be found, if only so I could learn the location of my keys. But I knew from my studies of the Cumberlands that a disappearance in these dread mountains meant an encounter with a whimpus, and I knew, from my research into the whimpus, that never would I see my nephew's face in God's sweet world again. So I located a reputable medium (no mean feat) and got her to call young Shagtemple on her Ouija-brand oracular board. From the board, from the medium, from Beauregard Shagtemple, I learned the horrible truth.

The six scouts, Shagtemple in the lead, had indeed gone hiking in an area that they should have clearly seen was marked with whirling whimpus spoor. They ignored the

doe-flavored syrup on the nearby trees. They ignored the distant droning sound, like a giant top, as it came closer and closer.

They were crouching down to smell a bloodflower (the state carnivorous flower of Tennessee) when the whimpus struck from behind. Three lads were turned into scout-batter before anyone knew what was happening. And then, remarkably, the whimpus stopped spinning.

Sightings of a whirling whimpus are exceptionally rare, and rarer still is a glimpse of the whimpus at rest. The fearsome creature resembles a large gorilla with extra-long arms and only one leg, which ends in a hoof. On this hoof it stands and spins. Beauregard Shagtemple and the two tenderfoots watched in awe as the whimpus, slowly and deliberately, licked the sticky remains of the their former comrades off its paws with a long, pimply tongue.

"Maybe it'll be full," one of the tenderfoots said.

But then the whimpus hopped up on its single hoof. It began to spin like a ballerina, faster and faster, until it became just a blur, and then a whir, which is the technical term for a blurred blur. Soon it was nothing more than a disturbance in the air rattling branches nearby and kicking up dust. The scouts ran,

but who can outrun a whirlwind?

They sowed the wind, and they were reaped.

Beauregard Shagtemple saw one tenderfoot go down, and then he stopped running. He saw a whirlwind ahead of him. When he turned to each side, and even behind him, there was a whirlwind there, too. He thought for a moment he was surrounded. But then he remembered what he'd learned earning his meteorology merit badge.

Cyclones and tornados whirl their winds around a central area of calm, called the eye of the storm. You can stand in absolute stillness and calm while all around you is whirling chaos: You are in the tornado's eye. And at that moment Beauregard Shagtemple could see that on every side the whirlwind whirled.

He realized that he was standing

safely at the very eye of the whimpus.

Then he realized that made no sense, and so he was turned to liquid.

A moment of silence, please, dear reader, for Beauregard Shagtemple. Worst of all, I learned he had my keys on him at the time, which means they were liquefied, too.

The last tenderfoot survived, incidentally, and staggered out of the woods weeks later, hale though quite mad. But who cares about that? Now I'll never get into my strongbox. And the creatures inside it are getting hungrier.

Acropelter

(Papio stretcharmstrongus)

The acropelter dwells high in the trees throughout the vast belt of lumberwoods that stretches across the northern part of the continent, feasting on woodpeckers and owls.

Some say the acropelter is not necessarily hostile to humanity and only attacks lumberjacks when they are chopping down the trees the acropelter calls home. These people are fools.

The acropelter is the largest New World monkey, closely related to the African baboon, but slightly more evil. Its arms are preternaturally long. The older the acropelter, the longer the arms—the longer the arms, the more elbows each arm has. It is disturbing to see an old acropelter with six or seven elbows in each arm swing disjointedly through the trees, stopping only to wrench a dead branch from a trunk and hurl it at a poor soul below.

As elementary knowledge of mechanics teaches us, the longer and bendier the arm, the more powerful its throw. The acropelter is therefore deadly when it hurls its missiles (occasionally rocks, but usually dead tree limbs). Those struck dead by the hurled branches are stashed in hollow tree trunks, where they are sometimes located by search parties or concerned relatives. The corpses, when dragged from the hollows, are always found to be missing their arms.

Lumberjack Ole Kittelson is one of the few to survive an acropelter attack. The acropelter that pegged him was a juvenile, with arms scarcely longer than a man's, and the branch it threw was particularly mealy and shattered to powder on Kittelson's hard dome. Kittelson purchased a motorcycle helmet, which he wore night and day, and became one of the first to study the acropelter in detail.

Kittelson began by prying through

innumerable dead
trees to find the
carcasses of acropelter
victims long undiscovered. The bodies were
never eaten—humans do not taste as sweet as
owls, nor as saltily delicious as woodpeckers'
tails—but the arms were always gone, bones
and all. To a man like Kittelson, dogged and
tough but not very bright, this was a mystery
he could not let go.

When no further clues were forthcom-
ing, Kittelson tried to interview acropelters.
He'd stand beneath their trees, helmet on.
"You have nothing to fear—I'm unarmed,"
he'd shout up at them, unaware of the grim
irony. "If you need anything, I'd be glad to
give you a hand." The fearsome creatures
would answer by pelting him with branches,
which bounced off his helmet and battered
the rest of his body.

Finally, an ancient acropelter swung over Kittelson. Its arms were at least twenty feet long, with as many joints as a squid's tentacle. It snapped off the largest, sturdiest tree branch it could find. Kittelson smiled up at the creature, and the creature smiled back. "I found his smile quite disarming," Kittelson later told me.

When the acropelter hurled the branch, its long arm cracked like a whip. The branch hit Kittelson squarely on the head and broke his helmet in half. He fell unconscious, but was not yet dead. He would be found an hour or so later, partially stuffed in a tree, weak from blood loss.

Both of his arms were missing.

When I interviewed Kittelson three days later, he told me all his secrets: that he had once kissed a dog on the lips, that he ate toothpaste like candy. "I care nothing about these things," I said. "Tell me of the acropelter."

He managed to choke out what he had seen. Knocked senseless by the acropelter's blow, he regained consciousness just as the enormous beast was tearing off his arms as though they were dead branches. Grabbing the limbs by their bloody sockets, the beast waved them around like pennants. Kittelson watched in horror as his disembodied hands began to flex and grasp with a life of their own. Slowly, the acropelter's hands fused to Kittelson's arms, its skin spreading and growing over the seam between them, the nerves and veins snaking forward to merge with these, its new limbs.

Kittelson now saw that the acropelter's long arms were a chain of human arms, each hand gripping the base of the next arm. Using Kittelson's former hands, the acropelter stuffed him in a hollow tree and took off into the forest.

The two halves of Kittelson's helmet were donated to the Smithsonian's cryptozoology wing.

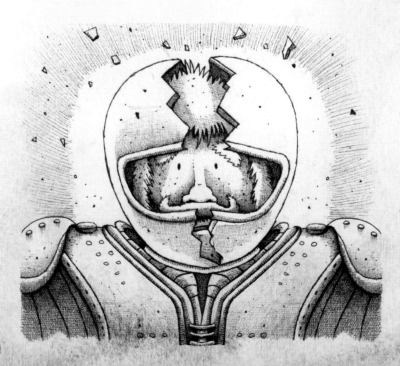

Hoop
Snake

(Orotundus velox)

Although Australia has the most dangerous snakes of any continent (one study claims
that 130 percent of Australian snakes are venomous, which sounds to me like a mathematical
error), North America comes a close second, with
the rattlesnake, the copperhead, the Wisconsin
python, the subterranean snake-man of Fairfield
County, the cottonmouth, and, deadliest of all,
the hoop snake.

The hoop snake is named for its unusual
method of locomotion: It grabs its tail in its jaws,
forming a hoop, and rolls by flexing its muscles
to adjust its center of gravity. On a clear, smooth
surface, the hoop snake can reach sixty miles per

hour. When it is pursuing prey, the snake is difficult to elude: If you leap over a fence to escape, dear reader, the snake just unhoops, crawls through the fence, and then rehoops on the other side.

What makes the snake truly terrifying is its virulent poison, which it keeps in a stinger in its tail.

Victims stung by the hoop snake rapidly turn purple, swell up, and die.

In 1869, geologist John Wesley Powell was stung in the right arm by a hoop snake while surveying the Grand Canyon. Powell immediately removed his right arm with a hatchet and cast it aside. The arm, even after amputation, continued to swell. A member of the expedition, William H. Dunn, poked the swollen limb with a stick, causing it to explode. Some of the tainted blood from the exploding arm hit Dunn in the eye; Dunn died in agony six days later (Powell survived).

Other memorable individuals killed by the hoop snake include Harriet Beecher Stowe, President Warren G. Harding, Kit Carson, the Lindbergh Baby (perhaps), and P. T. Barnum's beloved little circus performer Admiral Dot.

But the worst disaster, in terms of loss of human life, precipitated by the hoop snake was the notorious case of Edmund Virgil Bodenschantz, a farmer in now-defunct Oleander County, Maine. In 1865 he was hoeing his turnips when he saw a hoop snake rolling across the fields toward his hog pens. In a somewhat foolhardy display of bravado, Bodenschantz raced over to the hogs, brandishing his hoe, and caught the snake as it was slithering into the pigsty. During the brief but chaotic melee, Bodenschantz managed to decapitate the snake with the hoe, while the snake's own attack with its caudal stinger was luckily blocked by the hoe handle.

Immediately, Bodenschantz dropped the hoe, the handle of which had begun to swell. He fetched over some neighbors to witness the unprecedented phenomenon, so we do have several eyewitness accounts and one rough pencil sketch of the scene, made on the back of an envelope.

By nightfall, the hoe handle had swollen to the size of a small tree; by the next morning, it was the equivalent volume of about seventeen cords of wood. The split metal hoe head was still attached at one end, and the serpent's tail was embedded in the wood, pulsating eerily.

Bodenschantz tried to make the county fair circuit, displaying the headless hoop snake and the enormous swollen handle, but his story was rejected as implausible, and he was pelted with fruit and old patent medication bottles. The envelope with sketch was rejected as insufficient evidence. Seeking to make at least some money off the handle, he sold it as timber to a local toothpick conglomerate, Hygienic Best, which was able to turn the handle into some fourteen million toothpicks.

Unfortunately, the toothpicks were saturated with the

virulent poison of the hoop snake.

Eighteen thousand boxes of Hygienic Best toothpicks were recalled. Three boxes, however, made their way past the range of the recall; they had been ordered by the Mayor's Office in New York City, to be used at the annual Mayor's Gala (at 350 Fifth Avenue; by invitation only).

As the telegraph wires had been cut by savage Frenchmen, a Hygienic Best messenger (Mr. Jonathan van Oort) had to ride night and day from Maine to New York to explain the error. Fortuitously, Van Oort arrived at the Mayor's Gala just before the hors d'oeuvres were to be served. But at the

door the mayor's honor guards, dressed
as Prussian admirals, seized Van Oort; his
clothing, ragged and dusty from several
days' ride, was considered inadequately
festive for the Gala. They took him for a
beggar from the Bowery; or a ruffian from
Tammany Hall; or even a Brooklynite. They
struck him with truncheons and would not
listen to what he said. What he said was:

"You've got to let me in! Those toothpicks are venomous! They've been poisoned
by a hoop snake! In the name of this great
republic and its thirty-six states, you've got
to let me warn the mayor!"

"By invitation only," the guards replied,
with their truncheons.

Inside the mayor's mansion, though, his words came through only as the muffled and piecemeal cries of a madman. "Toothpicks . . . hoop snake . . . thirty-six!"

Colonel Benajah P. Bailey, retired, late of the 86th Infantry, had been bloviating to a circle of admirers about his campaigning at Fredericksburg when he heard these fragments. He set his snifter of brandy down on a silver tray and said, "Hoop snake, eh? Heard about one of those fearsome creatures outside of Chancellorsville. Stabbed a squirrel with its tail spike, it did, and started to swallow the poor varmint afore it had finished swelling. Stuck in that fool snake's throat and swelled it up like a balloon, until its gasket ruptured. It was the most repellent thing I ever saw, and I seen a man take a cannonball through his bosom at Gettysburg."

Caroline Astor said that such talk was vulgar, and wouldn't the colonel please try the canapés?

They were just coming around, on silver trays, each pierced by a festive toothpick.

The colonel took a canapé in hand, but he kept speaking, as he usually did. "Queer thing, the hoop snake. They say its poison is worse than a Frenchman's socks. Met a man from Texas once—a Union man, but from

Texas—told me a story about a rattlesnake they got down there. Said it was the most toxic of varmints. His story had it where a cowboy stepped on a rattler's head and died the same day. His boots, they got passed on to a friend.

"His friend put on the boots, also fell over dead.

"His son inherited, but he put on the boots and fell dead in his turn. Altogether five miserable cusses wore the boots and died afore anyone thought to look inside the boot. There, dadblastit, was a rattlesnake fang, jest stuck in the sole and poisoning anyone who put it on."

He raised the canapé to his lips, but there the colonel paused, as though lost in thought. It was the first time he had stopped talking (other than to take a sip of brandy) in seven hours. Outside the window a dim, mad voice could still be heard howling about toothpicks. The colonel said, "Them folk from Texas think everything in Texas is the biggest, the orneriest, and the dangerous-est. Five from one snakebite, that's no small shakes. But I'd like to see how many a good old hoop snake could get with jest one little sting. By gum, that I'd like to see!"

But he never did. For then Colonel Bailey popped the canapé in his mouth and fell over dead. All around him, as he would have noticed if he'd been the sort to pay attention, writhed the cream of New York society, over a thousand men and women swelling and bloating in their finery. Caroline Astor also broke a string of pearls, so the evening was a complete disaster.

In concession to the powerful toothpick lobby, Mayor Hoffman covered up the mass poisoning, blaming the deaths on cholera, but the Hygienic Best toothpick factory closed down regardless. No one would attempt to manufacture toothpicks in Maine for another twenty years. And on one night in New York there were 1,137 deaths from one snake's sting, a record that will probably never be bested, not even in Texas.

Snow Wasset

(Serpentoformus ferox)

The scariest things always dwell *underneath*. Underneath that rock over there crawl blind-worms and grubs and other foul creatures. Underneath the soil lurk the drow, slipping up to the surface world to steal human children. And underneath the drow loom fell caverns with ancient beings who have never seen the sun. Underneath the oceans the true masters of this world swell and burble. All of this is Cryptozoology 101. But what is rarely spoken of is what strange creature lives *underneath the snow*.

In the northern reaches of Canada, the undersnow is ruled by the savage wasset. Its kingdom is seasonal, and during summer months it crawls around bogs on stubby legs, estivating through the hottest period ("estivating" is the term for summer hibernation). When the snow begins to fall, the wasset sheds its legs like a bad haircut and begins a new life swimming under the snow. When man or beast passes above the wasset, it bursts through the snow crust, grabs its prey, and tunnels back under, leaving nothing behind but a hole in the snow and a few drops of blood.

The wasset is genuinely considered to be the second fiercest and toughest creature in North America, after the hodag. But because it lives in places sparsely inhabited and rarely visited, the wasset usually poses no danger to humans. However, the forbidding northern wastes of Canada have had their boom times: the Gold Rush of the 1890s, the Uranium Exploitation of the 1930s, and the Fluoride Excitement of the late 1990s. Times like these, the wassets feast.

In 1998 thousands of fluoride miners had thronged to the Arctic reaches around Great Bear Lake to seek their fortunes. One of those thousands was Khenbish McDouglas, a young man who had left a dull life as a starfish sharpener in Vancouver, dreaming of a northern paradise where the streets were paved with fluoride. Instead, he found a harsh, untamed, roadless land, where it was so cold that if you cut yourself shaving the blood came out in cubes. McDouglas joined a caravan of three dozen miners snowshoeing deeper into the wilds, in search of rich veins of fluoride to mine and ship to needy southern dentists.

McDouglas's caravan moved slowly, for it was bitter that winter. The thermometer read thirty below—if that thermometer had been an inch longer, everyone in the party would have frozen to death. And as the miners tramped across the blistering wastes, the sound of their snowshoes brought the wassets slithering like eels through the undersnow. The feasting of the wassets, when they struck, was horrific.

One by one, screaming miners would be pulled under the snow, out of sight and gone.

The miners could hear their comrades' bodies being devoured, right under their feet. They lost five good men that first day of the trek, and also Stinky Lou.

Each wasset, as it dragged a man down, stopped to feast on its prey. It is their usual custom to build a nest inside the corpse and devour it from the inside. As a grown man

will feed a snow wasset for about a week, the party should have had plenty of time to move on while the wassets dined. But still they were not safe; for one wasset proved cunning, and realized that if it killed more miners than it could eat, their corpses would stay fresh in that natural icebox that is the Northwest Territories; it could then dine all winter, at its leisure. And so every day, as they marched along, another miner would be sucked under the snow. The first half of every day was a time of stark terror for the miners, until the wasset struck and another one of their friends died. Only then could they breathe easily.

Sweat froze on Khenbish McDouglas's brow in the morning, and he would chip it off at night. He was not the only one sweating in terror. Even the bravest sourdough—as the miners were called—would not wish to be tracked day by day by a fearsome creature, hundreds of miles from civilization.

At night the miners would climb the great pine trees that dotted the area, for the wasset cannot climb. But morning always came, and morning brought death.

In desperation, the miners tried setting traps for the wasset, hunting local fauna—arctic porcupines or teacup wolverines—and hanging the game under deadfalls or over snares. The wasset claimed the bait, but it was so swift in striking that the deadfalls landed harmlessly behind it and the snares caught nothing but frozen chunks of air. And each day there were fewer and fewer miners left to set snares and hunt bait.

At last the wasset had brought the miners' numbers down to just four poor souls.

The four spent that long, bitter night in the trees weeping and wishing they were home.

They couldn't literally weep, of course; their tear ducts were clogged with ice. But they were pretty sad, nonetheless.

The next day brought better luck, though, and it was all thanks to Khenbish McDouglas, whose trap finally caught the beast. McDouglas had set a snare with a porcupine as bait, and he had accidentally hung his porcupine upside down. The snare was ineffective, but when the wasset leapt up to grab the porcupine, it swallowed the spiny beast hind end first.

Even a hodag would be discomfited, should it swallow a porcupine backward. The wasset choked for a while, rolling back and forth in the snow, and the miners all ran forward and battered it to death with shovels and picks.

Then they skinned the beast.

Because a wasset's hide has no armholes, it has long been desired by Native Americans as it makes excellent canoes. Similarly, the surviving miners (except for Stinky Lou's brother, Jim, whom they left behind) were able to stretch the hide around a frame to fashion a sled, which they rode down the indigenous luge trails back to Alberta. They no longer cared for fluoride mining—they wanted only to be somewhere warm and not dangerous. As they sailed along they ate wasset meat and clutched their weaponized shovels against any dangers that might come spiraling out of the dark. They ate heartily. By the time they coasted into Fort McMurray, all that was left of the wasset was its bones.

No fully intact wasset skeleton had ever been recovered, so McDouglas found himself possessed of a valuable property. He sold the skeleton to the Musée Canadien for a hefty sum. Craftsmen mounted the skeleton in the museum's cryptozoology wing. There was a ribbon-cutting ceremony, and Khenbish McDouglas was invited. It was a long way to come for a boy from small-town Vancouver.

Later, after the crowds thinned out, Khenbish McDouglas stood alone in the vast marbled hall, gazing upon the bones of the fearsome creature he had captured. He was a celebrity now, and would sharpen sea life no more. Was that pride he was exuding—pride in a job well done?

He heard it before he saw it.

The mounted skeleton of the snow wasset popped free of its moorings, one by one, and it sounded like popping corn. Khenbish McDouglas turned and saw the skeleton snaking toward him, its ribs clattering along the marble floor. It was only then that he realized: This whole time, *the wasset had just been playing possum.*

Central American Whintosser

(Helicoform mexicanus)

An ancient maxim, often attributed to the Chinese historian Sima Qian, holds that whatever runs can be snared, whatever swims can be netted, and whatever flies can be shot, but because no one knows how a dragon moves, no one knows how to catch one. The same may be said of the whintosser.

The whintosser's method of locomotion is improperly understood. It must involve legs, for the whintosser has twelve of them circling its body like spokes on a wheel. Its head and tail are attached to its body by ball-and-socket joints, so that whichever set of legs is down, the whintosser is always right side up. It can fall down a mountainside without getting dizzy, which is fortunate, for it often falls down mountainsides.

José Mariano Mociño was the first to describe the whintosser, circa 1798 in the Mexican state of Guerrero. "What a handsome animal!" he exclaimed, in Spanish, or perhaps French. The whintosser then beat him up, stole his compass, and ripped up his notes. This is the nature of the whintosser. It is an unpleasant nature.

Worse still, some whintossers have developed a taste for human flesh by eating Band-Aids. These man-eaters, or *menschenfresser* as the locals in Guerrero call them, crave nothing less than human meat, for the flesh of the human is the sweetest and juiciest of all meats.

A friend told me that.

I encountered the whintosser while exploring the Laguna Mountains of California in search of the wild plunkus with my manservant, Hans. We had thrown dice on the journey out to learn how our hunt would go, and they came up snake eyes every time. I figured it meant we'd never catch the plunkus, but we caught one easily; it turned out that "plunkus" is just another name for the dingmaul, an animal I've seen about a thousand times, so that was a great disappointment. It was while we were packing up camp and feeling blue that the whintosser attacked.

We had hired several native guides,

mostly surfers and out-of-work actors, and the whintosser instantly consumed them all. "Bummer," I heard one of them say, as Hans and I ran away.

I knew that most bullets go unnoticed by the whintosser, and the large Teflon-coated, elephant-maiming bullets we carried would only make it mad. "I think this one is a *menschenfresser*," I told Hans as we ran, but, of course, he did not speak Spanish. I wanted to point out that it was unusual to see a whintosser this far north, and speculate on its motives, but I decided I would be better off making a plan for escape. I distracted it for a few precious seconds by scattering Band-Aids behind me. Nevertheless, the

rolling, jouncing, inimitable gait of the *menschenfresser* whintosser had it gaining on us steadily. In rough terrain it ran its fastest, for it could jump in the air and, like a crooked quarter, always land up. With my diamond-sharp mind I also noticed that the whintosser instinctively scrambled about on whatever legs were touching the ground.

Thereupon I led Hans through a large hollow log I'd spotted lying near the trail.

The whintosser was close behind us, in the proverbial "hot pursuit," as we raced through the log, crouching and ducking our heads in the tight squeeze.

And here we experienced the very event I had been anticipating. In the narrow confines of the log, the whintosser's legs, for the first time in its life, all touched down simultaneously. Below, it felt ground; above, it felt ground; all around, the whintosser felt ground. It could not help itself; it began to walk, with its three sets of legs, in three separate directions. In doing so, it tore itself into three separate pieces. Each piece emerged from the log and scampered off in a different direction, going twenty or thirty yards before each of the creature's three parts collapsed in a pool of blood: one-third of the whintosser's blood per piece.

I had been busy sniffing out by divining rod the most effective path of escape, and so I did not witness the death of the whintosser myself; but Hans did. And I looked up in time to see Hans's own terrible fate.

I have seen, in my travels, what can happen to a man who tries to follow with his eyes two objects moving away from each other. One eye looks left, and one eye looks right, until the face begins to look like the face of a walleyed pike. Most men blink, and get off with nothing worse than a wicked headache, but a strong-willed man (Theodore Roosevelt was such a man) will find his eyes traveling in separate directions with sufficient velocity that they will either jump from his head or, if they are tightly secured in their sockets, tear his head in two. Off the coast of Thrace, I once encountered a harpy that became unmoored from its own reflection in the sea; a young Theodore Roosevelt, who was with me at the time, watched the harpy and its wayward reflection until his entire body was torn in two (he managed to survive, of course).

Hans was not so lucky that day. One of his eyes followed one piece of the sundered whintosser, and another eye must've followed another piece, or perhaps tried to follow two, for there were three whintosser pieces and he had but two eyes. Indeed, Hans's face quartered itself, smack down the middle and also across the eyeline, so that each eye fell into two limp pieces, like a bisected grape.

The four parts of his **head** struck the ground **right** in front of me.

My efforts to halt the migration and spread of the Central American whintosser are well known enough that I need hardly repeat them here. I have coordinated with the Mexican and United States governments. I have laid snares and piloted dirigibles. I have kept busy, and I do not think about what I saw.

But at night, in bed, the sight of Hans's four head quarters continues to haunt me; keeps me from sleep; drops into my dreams (when I finally do sleep) like pieces of hail, sending me shrieking back to consciousness and gnawing at my bedclothes.

I have seen a wasp laying its eggs in an orphan's eyes. I have seen two cannibals fight over seconds until there was only one cannibal. I have seen *The King in Yellow*, that accursed drama of doomed souls. I have seen a grown man fall into the pool of Scylla, and emerge covered with barking dogs—I mean his flesh literally turned into barking dogs, so that he was a man-shaped mass of barking dogs. I have seen some horrible things in my life, but nothing quite as horrible as the four pieces of Hans's skull.

For the whintosser, with its three sets of legs, ran in three directions. But Hans managed to split his head into four pieces. Three of those pieces were watching the whintosser, *but what was the fourth one looking at*? It is this thing, the fourth thing, the *quartum quid*, that I fear. Is that fourth thing alive or dead? Does that fourth thing thirst for revenge? I am safe from the three pieces of the dead whintosser,

but will I ever be safe from the fourth thing?

Some have told me that I am mad, that there is no fourth thing, but that makes it even more terrifying.

Even more terrifying, because how can I defend myself against *something that does not even exist*?

Billdad

(Castor saltissimus)

The werewolf is one of the most famous of all fearsome creatures, perhaps due to the number of American celebrities (Emily Dickinson, Henry Clay, Eli Whitney) who have succumbed to lycanthropy. But they are not the only creatures that perpetuate their existence with a bite. Vampires, once much fiercer than they are today, are another notorious example, as is the common mongoose, whose bite slowly transforms the unwary into a shriveled, hairy parody of a human, and thence into a full-fledged mongoose. Dante describes (in canto 25 of the *Inferno*) a serpent that can bite a man and then *switch bodies with him*. And then, reversing everything, there is the billdad.

The billdad's bite is scarcely dangerous to a human; it lacks even rudimentary teeth. As it dwells only in the isolated lake regions of Franklin County, Maine, little was known about the creature until the mid-nineteenth century, when Erasmus D. Prescott set up a steam-powered sawmill along the Fairbanks, a small Franklin County stream surrounded by good pine and spruce. "The enterprise did not prove a pecuniary success," as contemporary sources put it, for the mill consumed more trees in its steam furnace than it cut, but Prescott did manage to capture, in a fox trap, a strange animal that resembled a kangaroo with a broad, flat beaver's tail. He called it a "billdad," for reasons that will never be known, for one day, Prescott and his billdad disappeared. Concerned neighbors ransacked his house, but they found nothing of value. Dirty dishes were in the sink. Prescott's pajamas were still in the bed. He was never seen again.

The billdad, however, or at least *a* billdad, was spotted a few days later frolicking around the homestead of an H. W. "Excelsior" Priest, Esq., and family. It looked younger than it had before, and neighbors heard Priest remark that it certainly appeared appetizing, with its plump springy drumsticks and its fatty tail.

Priest's wife and six children were so sick of their diet of acorns and moss that nearly anything may have looked appetizing.

One fact remains unassailable: Shortly thereafter, the Priests were all gone, never again to be seen. "Must've moved away," said the neighbors, rooting through the belongings they'd left behind. They'd left a lot behind.

Out on nearby Little Kennebago Lake, the billdads hopped and flourished. "There sure be a passel of billdads 'round here," people would say that summer, the summer of 1888. They spoke in broad Maine accents, and were very colorful. "Look mighty toothsome, too." Addison McIntyre,

who'd bought the old Jeremiah Stinchfield place, managed to trap some of the creatures and brought billdad kebabs to the Saturday church picnic. Next day, there were a lot of empty pews in the church. Next day, there were a lot more billdads fishing in the lake.

By this point everyone around knew what was going on. They had the circumstantial evidence, of course; they also had the last entry in little Susie McIntyre's diary, which read, in part:

I think I am turning into a billdad I probably shouldn't have eaten all that billdad at the picnic.

Throughout Franklin County people swore off the consumption of billdad. Only problem was that everyone at the picnic had agreed (before their transformation) that roast billdad was about the tastiest thing they'd ever had. This was 1888, of course, before Oreos and MSG, when most food just tasted like wet cardboard; or maybe the billdad's flesh really was that sweet. Susie McIntyre's diary also read, "Billdad tastes better than apple pie made of wishes."

People would gather around the lake to watch the billdads fish. A billdad hunkered crouched on the shore until a fish came near the surface of the lake; then it would leap out across the water, twenty or thirty yards a leap, passing right over the fish and walloping it on its head with that flat beaver tail. The stunned fish was then easy pickings for the billdad. "Seems to be a good enough life," people said to each other. Their eyes darted back and forth. They licked their lips. Many already had their nets out. Apple pie made of wishes sounded mighty good. Franklin County was soon depopulated, and the billdads were clogging the ponds.

According to a Zoroastrian creation myth, back in the days of Mashya and Mashyana (the Adam and Eve of Zoroastrian tradition), babies tasted delicious, and the first couple would eat each and every child they birthed. It was a crisis, for no new humans lived past their infancy. Lest the human race begin and end with the first couple, their creator, Ahura Mazda, took away the savor of baby flesh. He made children taste so disgusting that Mashya and Mashyana would raise children and populate the world instead of eating them. But the savor that had tempted Mashya and Mashyana, that savor of primordial baby—that savor was still in the meat of the billdad. And Ahura Mazda did not work his miracles in Maine; so Governor Sebastian Streeter Marble had to step up.

Governor Marble had heard about the Franklin County atrocity and feared that gourmands from other parts of his great state might seek out billdad and become billdads in turn. He secretly imported a crew of Grahamites—a vegetarian cult from Massachusetts—and bade them travel to Franklin County with syringes and inject all the billdads they found with castor oil. This catch and release program resulted in a generation of foul-tasting billdads. The curious who came to Franklin County in search of a meal pronounced, as they underwent their transformation, that it had not been worth it at all. Many others were turned off by the horrible smell, and never even ate the meat they'd come for.

Soon Franklin was repopulated with humans, the locals shunned the billdads, and their population dropped off. If anyone ate a billdad again, it was no one very important or influential. The story of the delicious billdads was forgotten to all except those willing to slog through the secret memoirs of Sebastian Streeter Marble (such as yours truly, dear reader).

And I wondered: What if "billdad transformation" was strictly a local phenomenon; what if billdad meat, when exported from Franklin County, Maine, becomes harmless? There is precedent for food to have different effects in different regions: For example, if you eat human flesh in Canada, you become a wendigo, an accursed monster; while if you eat human flesh in Paris, you become president of France, if I understand their electoral process correctly. If billdad sausages could be sold everywhere *except* parts of Maine, that would still be a lot of sausage sales. I consider myself a man of independent means, and I do not wish to sound avaricious, but maintaining a cryptozoological garden requires funding that is difficult to acquire when so many of my visitors are eaten, mauled, poisoned, petrified, or have eggs laid under the skin. Every billdad sausage sale could help defray the cost of putting better locks on the shagamaw pit.

I sped to Maine and caught a billdad (rare and elusive as they now are). Then I sped to

Cusco, Peru, the furthest I could go from Maine without having to switch time zones and interfere with my carefully cultivated sleep schedule. The city of Cusco is near where guinea pigs were first domesticated, so it seemed a fine place to find a human guinea pig. I fried up some empanadas with billdad meat inside. "Would you like some free empanadas?" I asked a passerby. I tried to choose a passerby who looked like a scoundrel, so I wouldn't feel too bad if my experiment transformed him into a billdad.

He took two or three bites out of one empanada and then threw it on the ground. "It tastes like my butt," he said, or he may have. My Spanish is not so good. Anyway, I already said he was a scoundrel.

"Possible it could use some seasoning," I thought, and absentmindedly popped a spare piece in my mouth. It was quite good, and tasted like chicken. Only after I'd polished off the empanadas did I realize *I had tasted billdad meat.*

I did not wish to become a billdad! I don't know how to swim, and I would find life as a billdad unpleasant. But, as the long seconds of anxiety ticked away without my legs elongating, I decided that the experiment had been a success. I headed back toward my hotel, congratulating myself on a job well done. I cast one last look over my shoulder as I went, and that's when I saw the scoundrel who had rejected my empanadas—I saw him suddenly melt away into three rats connected at the tails. The rats scampered down a Cusco alley that was six centuries old. And I ran away, too.

Now I lie here in bed at night, trembling with dread and anticipation. Every nervous twitch makes me think I'm splitting into rats. Every squeal and creak of my manor house makes me worry that these are squeaks from my own tiny voice boxes. I think I'm starting to grow feathers, but that could be unrelated. I know that at any moment the horrible transformation could begin, like a second puberty; and one was enough. *Perhaps,* I tell myself, *that jerk could turn into three rats anyway.* It seems like the kind of thing a scoundrel like him would do. But really, when I look at this rationally, what are the odds that the *one human* I fed my billdads to was capable of such a feat?

I have run the numbers, and the odds are *less than one in fourteen.*

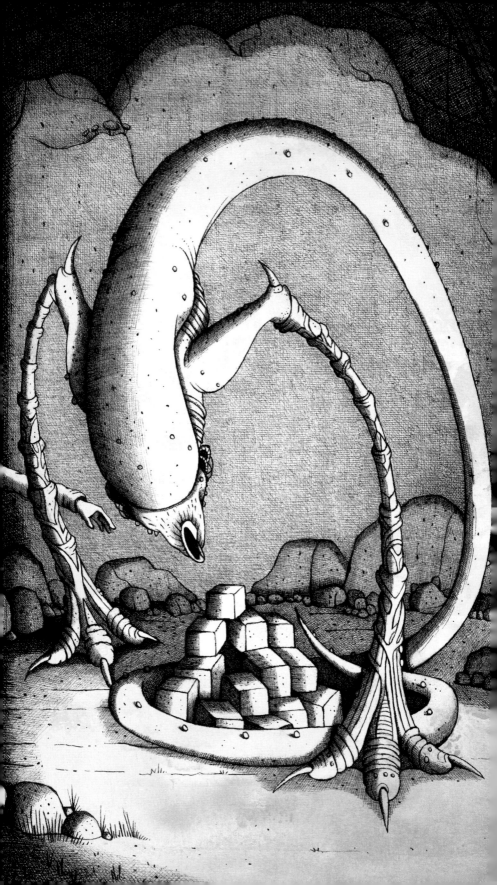

Tripodero

(Bertha magna)

For three days my study smelled of tobacco smoke. I opened the windows and sprayed civet musk liberally, but the smell just got worse. Then one day, as I was poring over volumes of forgotten lore, my old colleague Ludvík Ctvrtlik strode through the door. He was smoking a pipe. "You can't smoke in here," I said.

"Don't worry," he told me. "This is time smoke. It travels backward in time, so the smell doesn't linger. As soon as I leave the room you won't smell a thing."

"But that means that for the last few days—" I began, but he hushed me with a wave of his pipe. He had come with other plans. He wanted to enlist my help in securing the eggs of the tripodero.

The tripodero is one of the most mysterious species on the North American continent, and one of the most dangerous. It is the world's largest land echinoderm—echinoderms being the strange phylum of creatures that includes the starfish, the sea cucumber, and William Wordsworth. Of all invertebrates they are the closest relatives to humans, but their thought processes are the most difficult to understand. No one has ever reasoned with a starfish. And no one has ever stolen a tripodero's eggs.

Ctvrtlik extracted a small-scale model of a tripodero from his carpetbag. It was made of brass, but was otherwise very lifelike. Easy to see were the tripodero's most distinguishing features: two long telescoping legs that permit the creature to change its height radically. These, along with its prehensile, tentacle-like tail, put the "tripod" in "tripodero." In the mountainous chaparral thickets of California, where the tripodero lives, these legs can telescope up to ten feet in length, or shrink back down to almost nothing, allowing the creature to tower over the bush or slink underneath it.

But this is not what makes the tripodero dangerous.

The head of the tripodero is almost featureless except for a puckered mouth, from which it is capable of expelling sharp, rock-hard "teeth" with the force of a cannon. It seems to regrow the teeth quickly, or at least no tripodero has ever been found to run out. And the force with which it fires these teeth can penetrate even an armored tank, or the skin of a whintosser.

"We're both going to die,"

I told him; but Ludvík Ctvrtlik had come prepared. He possessed a device powered partly by the philosopher's stone and partly by steam, which was capable of throwing up a kinetic suppressor shield in front of us; the tripodero could fire all the teeth it wanted at us, yet we would be safe.

I hope I have drawn a sufficiently accurate character of myself that it is clear I am always up for adventure, especially if it involves stealing things from a poor dumb animal. Just to be sure, I diced for the success of the mission and threw snake eyes every time. But I'm always throwing snake eyes over California. Probably the dice are loaded.

Getting to the West Coast was easy enough (there is a secret passage through the conservatory), but our trek through the mountains contained enough adventures to fill a volume in the life of Baron Trenck. There were lava flows and ice floes and sentient waterfalls and salamanders made of glass. There was a labyrinth fashioned completely out of blood, with *the void* in its center and the only exit through a needle's eye. There was also a gift shop that sold hot chocolate, so it wasn't all bad. And finally, on torn and bleeding knees we crawled over a ridge and saw before us a cache of tripodero eggs.

Tripodero eggs are cubes, so they don't roll down the slopes and off the cliffs of the scrub mountains. Whether they are laid square or come out round and are later squared off, like the baby in the *Honcho Gusho Shinshi* who was placed in a box until it developed corners, is subject to debate. What is not subject to debate is that the eggs are jealously guarded by an adult tripodero, always on the lookout for any mischief. This tripodero strolls around on its long legs, presumably searching for food, and by all appearances not paying attention to the eggs.

But anyone approaching too close just gets gunned down, a tripodero tooth smack between the eyes.

We saw no tripodero around, but this meant nothing. The eggs would not be unguarded.

Undismayed, Ludvík Ctvrtlik brought out the mechanism for his kinetic suppressor shield. We turned the crank and fiddled with the dials. When all was ready, Ctvrtlik carried the device and I carried the sack, and we ran forward. The kinetic suppressor shield was invisible (of course), so I could only take it on faith that it was working. I knew that I was gambling not only with my own life but also with the lives of all the parasites that throve inside my guts; tripodero eggs, however, were worth the gamble. Not only was it necessary for scientists to study their shape and taste, but also my collection felt incomplete without at least one. Where other eggs rolled around willy-nilly, the tripodero egg could sit flat on a desk, and even be used as a paperweight. I tried to think of the eggs' utility and charm, and not of the mortal danger in which I was placing myself and my intestinal leeches.

For indeed, no sooner had I started shoveling eggs into the sack than a distant rustling in the chaparral indicated the awareness of an adult tripodero. With a bizarre slide-whistle sound, the fearsome creature suddenly telescoped up from out of the brush a hundred yards off. An unearthly keening was its only warning. Then it began to fire. There was a puff from the sphincteral cannon of its mouth and the crack of the sound barrier being blown through as a tooth came rocketing toward us.

This was the moment of truth. Perhaps I paused in filling the sack. Afraid for its life, a tapeworm I'd harbored for several years evacuated my body and crawled a rather filthy trail across the rocks, seeking a safer host. But in general I was resolute.

Any conventional shield, even one seven ox hides thick, would have been sundered by one blow of that tooth. But a kinetic suppressor absorbs kinetic energy, and it grows stronger the more force is thrown at it. The tooth struck the shield, slowed to an abrupt stop, and then fell harmlessly to the ground.

"It's working," Ctvrtlik shouted, like a dimwit.

It was the work of a moment to finish stowing the eggs, sixteen in all. Four or five more booming sounds, and when I looked up several more teeth were tumbling down, halted by the kinetic suppressor. There was also a tripodero stalking across the brush at us on its ten-foot-long legs. We started to run, but we were hampered by the encumbrance of my sack, and by Ctrvtlik's need to keep his device angled such that the kinetic suppressor and its invisible shield were behind us. I gave a little hop to avoid stepping on my old friend the tapeworm. If we had to run through chaparral, we would have been caught in an instant, but we ran in the other direction, up a rough path to a craggy peak. The tripodero's legs could not bend in the way needed to clamber up after us. We stood there, on the peak, looking at the rough ground we'd just scrambled across, over at an utterly alien face that nevertheless radiated despair. The tripodero turned away from us, perhaps (we thought) in shame.

And then its legs, already ten or twelve feet long, began to extend further. It rose higher and higher, until it must have been twenty feet off the ground.

The legs tapered to pencil slimness, and the whole body swayed in the gentle breeze.

Still looking away from us, it angled its snout and fired.

"I wonder what it is shooting at now," Ctvrtlik said, straining his eyes. These were his last words, for just then a tooth struck him from behind, emerging from his forehead right between the eyes. He crumpled to the ground, dropping the kinetic suppressor, which shattered. The tripodero didn't know the shield was down, of course, and it was preparing to fire again, the long way around the earth, when I hallooed and set the sack down, gently, displaying the eggs. With fishing wire I lowered the sack from the peak, letting it rest on a soft shrub. As the tripodero moved to reclaim its eggs, I split for the hills. Piranha-buzzards had already stripped Ctvrtlik's body to a skeleton, but I did take his philosopher's stone. I also had three tripodero eggs, which I had secreted under my hat. For I knew the tripodero, like all echinoderms, could not count past twelve. It would never even know these were gone.

You can see them on my desk. I'm hoping they'll hatch.

Hyampom Hog Bear

(Ursus curare)

The Hyampom hog bear gets its name not from its pug, swinish nose (which it nevertheless possesses) but rather from its diet.

The mountains of Hyampom, California, are verdant with oak trees, the acorns of which make delectable pig fodder. Consequently, there have long been a large number of hog ranches in the area, their pig drifts running free, feasting on acorns and awaiting the roundup. "Can't wait for the roundup," the pigs may whisper to each other, for, being pigs, they are too stupid to understand that the roundup will spell their conversion into sausage. But sulking along these same mountains is the hog bear, hankering for a roundup of its own.

As the hog bear is an elusive creature, its existence was first deduced only by the carnage it left behind. Swineherds patrolling the mountains would hear pained squealing, and, ascending to investigate, come across whole drifts of pigs, each one with an enormous chomp taken out of its fatty back. Not only was the chomp painful to the pig in question but also the bacteria in the bear's filthy mouth would infect the wound, tainting the taste of the pig flesh such that it could only be used in bologna or chewing gum, and not in any high-grade meats. Perhaps this is the reason the hog bear takes only one bite out of each pig—the second bite tastes skunky.

Or perhaps pigs are like apples, and the first taste is always the sweetest.

Regardless of motive, the hog bear's actions had the unfortunate result of spoiling the whole drift of pigs, when one pig could have satisfied the appetite of a bear this size.

Although the swineherds and hog ranchers of Hyampom usually encourage an all-pork diet, the hog bear's habit of not paying for the pigs it consumes was universally condemned by the American Ham Association. What they could not agree on, though, was what to do about the situation. Keeping the pigs penned up would be prohibitively expensive, as would multiplying the number of swineherds on guard. Injecting the pigs with foul-tasting castor oil (the "billdad gambit") would have ruined them for the market. One enterprising rancher, Marcus Wasselbaum by name, dressed his

pigs in cheap human clothes, with wigs and a touch of mascara, to deceive the bears, which worked temporarily.

Eventually a hog bear caught on, and one day swineherds came across a whole drift of bleeding pigs in prom dresses and tracksuits, each with a missing chunk of back flesh; their wigs slipped askew; their mascara running. Ursodental experts determined that all the bite marks came from the same set of jaws. Psychiatrists agreed that no one who witnessed the scene should be allowed to own knives or operate heavy machinery.

Why didn't the pigs scatter when the hog bear came near? How was a lone hog bear able to take one bite out of twenty or thirty pigs in succession? These mysteries remained unsolved, even as scientists collected hog bear footprints and hog bear spoor and sold hog bear merchandise.

"I bet the hog bear is just a fat hairy guy who likes bacon," said President Truman. "Everyone likes bacon." But President Truman was wrong.

By the late '60s the hog bear problem had reached a crisis level. California was in danger of losing its pork production to fish-fed pigs raised on rafts floating in the Pacific, and those hog bears weren't helping. The American Ham Association hired Eugene S. Bruce, Jr., of the U.S. Forest Service, one of the few men to have seen a hog bear in the wild, to advise them. Bruce tried hunting and trapping, but he had the most success with "beating parties"—large groups of people banging tambourines and drums to scare the hog bears away to another county. Some brought electric guitars with portable amps; some brought saxophones. After six months, and great expense, most of the bears had fled in terror from the noise, and the pigs looked safe.

But one particularly wily and potentially deaf bear remained behind, and with all his competition gone he was really able to run wild. Ursodental experts were able to confirm that all the damage was done by only one bear—the same one, incidentally, as the one from the Wasselbaum incident— but all the experts, even Bruce, were out of ideas on how to stop him.

I may have weighed in with a couple of suggestions. "Eugene," I may have said, "if this bear of yours is not scared of loud noises, perhaps you can scare him with loud clothing." I suggested checkered polyester Sansabelt slacks and a Hawaiian shirt with pictures of car crashes. Or I *may have suggested*—my lawyer is very clear on this point.

Somehow, with or without my input, Bruce struck upon the idea of employing the great quick-change artist Walter Fitzwalter. Fitzwalter had gained some notoriety in recent years dressing as jazz musicians and hippies and infiltrating terrorist groups for the FBI, but his real skill lay in his ability to change his appearance rapidly—from a businessman to a cheerleader to a Mongolian horseman in traditional garb. He had invented a device, which I had not assisted him with, that would automatically change his clothes, with tiny robotic arms, at the press of a button, and almost faster than the human eye can see. He could be anyone. And Bruce hired him to amble through the Hyampom woods, switching back and forth between an orange and pink striped muumuu and a silk Cuban shirt plus six-inch-wide tie with a hand-painted Hawaiian dancer. A neon stretch top with polka-dot leggings and teddy-boy ruffled shirt slash purple Edwardian velvet coat ensemble. A mustard plaid leisure suit and a leopard-print floor-length gown. Walter Fitzwalter, quick-change artist extraordinaire and not a bad guy, really, was the loudest thing in Hyampom that fall.

Science has marched on since the late '60s, and although we've forgotten some things, such as how to get to the moon, we have learned many others. We now know that the hog bear is capable of producing a musk that paralyzes the muscular system in both warm-blooded animals and Frenchmen. The occasional hunter had reported similar symptoms, which had been passed off as the side effects of snacking on poisonous berries. A concentrated dose can fully paralyze the diaphragm, causing the lungs to stop working and the victim to asphyxiate, but even in smaller doses the musk will induce sufficient weakness to prevent flight, which explains how one creature could bite so many successive hogs. Also, the hog bear can move backward and forward in time and can appear in multiple places at once.

This discovery has helped us untangle the tragedy of what happened that autumn day. The hog bear never attacks hunters, of course, or humans at all—it eats pigs, and sometimes acorns. But Walter Fitzwalter was dressed so outlandishly that the hog bear may have been reminded of Marcus Wasselbaum's disguised pigs that it had feasted on so long ago. It released its musk, paralyzing poor Fitzwalter as he ambled through the forest in surfer trunks and a rhinestone cape. And it took a bite.

Only one bite, for the hog bear always takes only one bite. One bite is not so bad.

But then Fitzwalter's automatic clothes-changing machine activated its little robot arms. The sequined vest disappeared to be replaced with a saffron smoking jacket. Intrigued by what appeared to be a whole new creature lying helpless before it, the bear returned for just one more bite. It must have been very painful, but it was hardly fatal.

And then his clothes changed again.

Seventeen outfits, all of dubious taste, Fitzwalter went through until there was not enough left of him to drape clothes on. When they found his jigsaw puzzle of a body, surrounded by the wispy remains of feather boas and artificial leather, some people claim Fitzwalter managed to gasp out my name and a call for revenge before dying. But my lawyer says this never happened.

There are still a few pig farms in Hyampom. There are still a few hog bears, too.

Appendix

FEARSOME FACTS

*not to scale

SLIDE-ROCK BOLTER
Habitat: Mountains
Range: Colorado
Height: 20' *
Weight: >25,000 lbs.
Diet: Whatever's in its path
Number of limbs: 3?
Life span: 80+ years
Ground speed: 65 mph
Fearsomeness: 9
Absurdity: 8

HODAG
Habitat: Lumberwoods
Range: Michigan
Height: 8' at shoulder
Weight: 3,000 lbs.
Diet: Carnivorous
Number of limbs: 4
Temperament: Fearsome
Life span: Death fears the hodag
Ground speed: 35 mph
Fearsomeness: 12
Absurdity: 4

TOTE-ROAD SHAGAMAW
Habitat: Lumberwoods
Range: Maine,
eastern Canada
Height: 7'
Weight: 900 lbs.
Diet: Garbage; me
Number of limbs: 4
Life span: 20–30 years
Ground speed: 35 mph
Fearsomeness: 10
Absurdity: 7

GUMBEROO
Habitat: Rain forest
Range: Washington,
Oregon
Height: 8'
Weight: 350 lbs. starving
Diet: Literally omnivorous
Number of limbs: 13
Life span: 4–7 years
Ground speed: 150+ mph
Hibernation period:
47–50 weeks a year
Fearsomeness: 9
Absurdity: 12

TERRASHOT
Habitat: Desert
Range: California/
Nevada border
Height: 6–8'
Weight: 80–120 lbs.
Diet: Herbivorous
Number of limbs: 3–7
Life span: Mysterious, ending
in loud bang
Ground speed: 1 mph
Fearsomeness: 5
Absurdity: 10

162

Habitat: Swamps and
wetlands
Range: Florida, Georgia,
and Louisiana
Height:
Weight: 3,000 lbs.
Diet: Umbrivorous
Number of limbs: 0
Activity cycle: Diurnal
Life span: 30–50 years
Fearsomeness: 8
Absurdity: 6

Habitat: Lumberwoods
Range: Wisconsin,
Minnesota, Ontario, and
Manitoba
Height: 13' at shoulder
Weight: 5,000–6,000 lbs.
Diet: Bark, pine needles
Lip: Pendulous
Number of limbs: 4
Life span: 20–30 years
Ground speed: 25 mph
Fearsomeness: 3
Absurdity: 6

HUGAG

Habitat: Lumberwoods
Range: Cumberlands
Armspan: 95"
Height: 8' at shoulder
Weight: 250–300 lbs.
Diet: Gooövorous
Number of limbs: 3
Life span: 11–17 prime years
Ground speed: 30–50 mph
Fearsomeness: 10
Absurdity: 11

WHIRLING WHIMPUS

Habitat: Scrubland
Range: California
Height: 2–10'+
Weight: 10 lbs.
Subphylum: Triplozoa
Diet: Detritivorous
Number of limbs: 2
Temperament: Inscrutable
Life span: 200 years+
Ground speed: 20 mph
Fearsomeness: 9
Absurdity: 10

Habitat: Desert
Range: Mojave
Height: 5' at shoulder
Weight: 120 lbs.
Diet: Tears, maybe?
Temperament: Hostile
Number of limbs: 4
Life span: Immortal?
Ground speed: 90 mph
Fearsomeness: 9
Absurdity: 8

ROPERITE

Habitat: Mountainous
forest
Range: Klamaths
Length: 50–80"
Weight: 150–300 lbs.
Diet: Hogs, pigs, oinkers,
and swine
Temperament: Fair
Number of limbs: 4
Life span: 18–25 years
Ground speed: 30 mph
Fearsomeness: 4
Absurdity: 5

HYAMPOM HOG BEAR

CROPELTER
Habitat: Lumberwoods
Range: Northern United States
Height: 4'
Weight: 50–80 lbs.
Diet: Woodpeckers and owls
Number of limbs: 4–20+
Temperament: Mean
Life span: 100–120 years
Tree speed: 35 mph
Fearsomeness: 8
Absurdity: 9

WHINTOSSER
Habitat: Mountains
Range: Mexico, California
Length: 4'
Weight: 70 lbs.
Diet: Carnivorous
Number of limbs: 12
Temperament: Disagreeable
Life span: 4–10 years
Ground speed: 15 mph
Fearsomeness: 8
Absurdity: 8

CACTUS CAT
Habitat: Desert
Range: Sonora, Arizona; New Mexico
Length: 3'
Weight: 25 lbs.
Diet: Cactus sap; cactus mice
Activity cycle: Nocturnal
Temperament: Intemperate
Ground speed: 15 mph
Life span: 15–25 years
Fearsomeness: 6
Absurdity: 4

SNOW WASSET
Habitat: Taiga
Range: Northern Territories
Length: 4–5'
Weight: 40–60 lbs.
Diet: Carnivorous
Number of limbs: 0 or 4
Temperament: Hungry
Activity cycle: Diurnal
Life span: 5–13 years
Ground speed: 35 mph
Fearsomeness: 8
Absurdity: 6

WAPALOOSIE
Habitat: Lumberwoods
Range: Washington, British Columbia
Length: 40"
Weight: 2–4 lbs.
Diet: Innocent canopy fungus that has never hurt anyone
Number of limbs: 4
Life span: 7–10 years
Fearsomeness: 1
Absurdity: 5

HOOP SNAKE
Habitat: Lumberwoods
Range: Grand Canyon to Maine
Length: 60–70"
Girth: 7"
Weight: 4 lbs.
Diet: Carnivorous
Number of limbs: 0
Life span: 15–30 years
Ground speed: 60 mph
Hibernation period: October–March
Fearsomeness: 9
Absurdity: 7

FEARSOME FACTS

BILLDAD
Habitat: Lakes
Range: Franklin County, Maine
Height: 30"
Weight: 35 lbs.
Diet: Fish
Activity cycle: Diurnal
Life span: 25 years
Flavor: Sweet; delicious
Ground speed: 30 mph
Fearsomeness: 2
Absurdity: 7

LEPROCAUN
Habitat: Mouseholes; outskirts
Range: Not Ireland
Height: 3' plus hat
Weight: 30 lbs. dry, 55 lbs. drunk
Diet: Facial features; whiskey
Activity cycle: Nocturnal
Temperament: Bitter
Life span: 10–15 years
Fearsomeness: 8
Absurdity: 7

SQUONK
Habitat: Mountains
Range: Poconos
Height: 2' at shoulder
Weight: 30–40 lbs.
Diet: Pus
Number of limbs: 3½
Temperament: Morose
Ground speed: 15 mph
Life span: Interminable
Fearsomeness: 11
Absurdity: 10

LUMBERJACK
Habitat: Lumberwoods
Range: United States
Height: 5'10"
Weight: 190 lbs.
Diet: Flapjacks
Number of limbs: 4
Life span: 55 years
Fearsomeness: 2
Absurdity: 1

SURVIVOR BUNNY
Habitat: Lumberwoods
Range: Lumberwoods
Length: 14"
Weight: 4–6 lbs.
Diet: Herbivore
Number of limbs: 4
Lifespan: 9–12 years (optimal conditions)
Ground speed: 35 mph
Fearsomeness: 10
Absurdity: 7

For Those Wanting More . . .

If you want to learn more about cryptozoology, the best but most dangerous method is to take to the field and seek out some fearsome creatures in the wild. Bring a flamethrower and a lucky rabbit's foot. Write a will.

For those who wish to stay alive and sane, another option is to read books about cryptozoology. The best book on the subject is this one, so you're halfway there. Also of great merit is the pioneering 1910 work by William T. Cox; it is also called *Fearsome Creatures of the Lumberwoods* (Press of Judd and Detweiller, Inc.), and this book is more or less an updating of the lore discovered by Cox. (Readers should be aware that the book contains racism above and beyond what one might expect from that era and approach it accordingly.) All North American cryptozoologists are walking in Cox's footsteps; sometimes literally, because he dug so many pits there is only one safe passage through. Cox's *Fearsome Creatures of the Lumberwoods* is out of print and hard to find, but you can read it for free online.

In 1939 Henry H. Tryon wrote his own update of Cox, called *Fearsome Critters* (The Idlewild Press), with illustrations by his wife. This book is also out of print and hard to find, but fortunately it is also freely available online.

The inimitable Richard M. Dorson studied the secret lore of North America in many fields; his work on cryptozoology, however, is best summed up in *Man and Beast in American Comic Legend* (Indiana University Press, 1982). Many of Dr. Dorson's books are still in print and easily locatable: *Man and Beast in American Comic Legend* is an exception.

There are many collections of "tall tales," which is what the superstitious and ignorant call scientific data; however, few of these collections focus on fearsome creatures. One that has more than its fair share of fearsomeness in it is Vance Randolph's *We Always Lie to Strangers* (Greenwood Press, 1974). This book is almost impossible to acquire.

Some of the most fearsome creatures live far outside of the lumberwoods. Europe, for example, has creatures so tough they can survive the metric system. Finding books about Old World monsters is about *ten thousand times easier* than finding any of the books listed above. You literally would need to be an illiterate savage not to find a dozen good books about unicorns and sphinges by groping at random, blindfolded, in your average bookstore. There are so many of these books, and they multiply at such a rate, that creeks and cisterns become choked and dammed with their waterlogged carcasses.

But there is still much that can be learned from them, and no cryptozoologist can be considered truly cultured without the knowledge they contain. The oldest books are the best: Pliny's *Natural History*, Aelian's *De Natura Animalium*, various medieval bestiaries (T. H. White translated one admirably as *The Book of Beasts*), and Thomas Browne's *Pseudodoxia Epidemica* are all easy to find, and reward careful study. Just skim the boring parts.

Jorge Luis Borges, the greatest writer of the twentieth century not to die in a madhouse, co-wrote with Magarita Guerrero a book that happily bridges the two worlds, old and new. *A Book of Imaginary Beings* includes fearsome creatures from several continents, and the hodag gets to rub shoulders with the harpy at last.

—Hal Johnson